LEGEND OF THE CORE:

The Core Elementalists

(Book 1: The Discovery of Elements)

Created By:

Kristopher Jackson & Zachary Scott

Dedication

IN REMEMBRANCE OF A PRINCESS
This is dedicated to you, Christina. Not a day goes by that I don't miss you, so I put my heart and soul into this masterpiece, in your name.

-Kris

Acknowledgements

Thank you to my mom, who never stopped believing in me. Doing pretty much all of this for you, so you're welcome.

Thank you to my older brother Lexx for helping me to understand that I'm great, no matter what anyone else says or thinks. It takes a god to mold a goat. Thank you to my older sister, Mairiah, for showing me that you have to put 100% greatness into everything. You're still clumsy, though.

Thank you to my younger sister Racheal for opening my eyes and showing me that strength and brilliance go hand in hand. You've gotta big head and I love you. Thank you to the few adults that I actually look up to, who taught me more about myself than I knew possible. Thank you to my brothers, who were fine with me being a nobody, but are that much prouder that I'm a somebody. Finally, thank you to all of the people who doubted and underestimated me and thought I'd always be a nobody... You probably need to think again.

- Kris

THE PROLOGUE

Think long and hard, then tell me, what do you believe in?
Do you think there could be life on other planets?
What about a God or an all-powerful entity?
Do you believe in titans? What about superheroes?
Tell me, do you believe in legends?

Greatness. A word with so much power that it bears the
heaviest of burdens.
Destiny. A word that holds so much hope but stirs the
worst of fears.
Hero. A word, when heard, instills an overwhelming sense
of protection and pride but also a layer of danger, change,
and heartbreak.

If you were given abilities and destined for greatness, do
you think that you would be prepared to accept the
responsibility?
Everything you thought you knew would be shifted into the
realm of impossibility with no warning.
Your life would completely change, and you'd be faced with
two sets of choices.

Acceptance or Denial.
Good or Evil.

Which would you choose?

1

ҬHOSE STUPID GEMSTONES

◇ What Are These? ◇

10:15 AM
Winifred Caverns

Dr. Arthur Arkaine, a tall Hispanic archaeology teacher, stood in front of his class, rattling off the names of his students, simultaneously taking roll and assigning them into groups. He pushed his fingers through his thicket of oil black hair and took a deep breath. He'd taken his class of thirty-two on a field trip to cave ruins to study rock formations, as he had been doing for the past twelve years. He looked down at his class attendance sheet and then back up at the students. Four kids were standing next to each other, chatting it up as they usually did in his class.

A light-skinned boy with an uncontainable mess of curly hair was the leader of the group. He was a few inches taller than everybody else and by far the most obnoxious. JJ Rodriguez. His multi-colored eyes caught the sunlight and drew you into whatever nonsense he was babbling on about. That boy had a need to always be talking about something and hardly ever shut up once he got started. Next to him was his tall, greenish-blue-eyed, caramel-complexioned accomplice, Charlotte Santiago. She had a beautifully sculpted face and auburn hair that was draped across her shoulder in a ponytail. The very end of it had been dyed three different colors: green, blue, and purple. It was strangely mesmerizing and called on your eyes to stare. She looked fairly exhausted with whatever JJ was saying, as she usually was. She stood next to her best friend, Cinthya Thompson, who insisted that anyone who crossed her path call her Cindy and nothing else. Cindy's hair stuck out just as much as Charlotte's, but in an entirely different way. The right side of her head was shaved completely bald, and led into a head full of wavy golden hair that was also pulled into a ponytail for the trip. Her fuchsia-dyed tips whipped around behind her in the warm dusty wind. That last member of the group was the shortest and the youngest and had a head full of gray hair since birth. Jericho Umpter stood to the left of JJ, the two of them were practically brothers and inseparable. Jericho had ash gray eyes to match his ash gray hair, which stuck out against his mocha colored skin. The four of them were so deep in conversation that they barely heard when Dr. Arkaine called their names.

"J. Rodriguez, C. Santiago, C. Thompson, and J. Umpter, you'll be in a work group for this assignment. Please be careful and remember who your partners are, which shouldn't be a problem for The Brady Bunch," he remarked.

Charlotte rolled her eyes at the comment, and a few of their classmates giggled at the joke.

"They are your teammates and potential lifelines. Be safe; JJ. Be mindful. Stay on topic; JJ. Be cooperative with one another and have fun," Dr. Arkaine instructed although his tone didn't match his message. "These are some old cave sites, so please have a little caution. Report back in an hour with any findings," he said and dismissed them.

"Let's get down in the dirt! Whoo!" JJ yelled as he rushed down into the cave mouth, helmet flashlight glowing.

"Boys," Charlotte and Cindy both mumbled under their breath.

"Okay, everybody. I really think we should be extra careful. These caves are old, I'm pretty sure Arkaine said," Jericho said after they'd been walking for a few minutes, trying to recall their teacher's instructions.

"Jericho, you gotta quit worrying so much, bro. You gotta be chill, the way the babes like it, like me," JJ said, trying his best to sound suave.

"How come you don't have a girlfriend then, JJ?" Charlotte questioned.

"Stop playin'. Charlie baby, you know you want this," JJ said in a cholo-like accent.

"She's not into the empty-headed ones. You know it's too bad. If she were, then you'd be number one on the list," Cindy rudely explained.

"Whatever. Let's just get dirty, er, working," he said, looking away, somewhat offended.

They all proceeded to descend further into the cave. They found a decent mining point and began working. It didn't take very long for the cave to be filled with metallic clanking from their pickaxes. Sweat beaded everyone's faces as the cave's humidity made itself known. It only took about twenty minutes before Charlotte had had her fill of its climate.

"This is so hard and incredibly boring," she complained. "Can we just leave and report we found nothing?"

"Why choose an archaeology elective if you didn't want to do any hard work?" Jericho asked.

"It seemed fun at the time, Je-ri-cho. Plus, all of you guys were doing it, so I thought it'd be a good idea, gosh," she retorted.

"Excuse me. It was just a question. No need to get in your feelings about it," he replied with a small grin tugging at the corner of his mouth.

They gave each other sarcastic looks, then turned around and began working again. Behind them, JJ was steadily going through the motions, enjoying the mess that accompanied the work. As he was striking the crumbling rocks, he noticed a strange glow. It was there for only a second. He thought about voicing his observation, but quickly withdrew the idea, feeling it wasn't of too much importance. His pickaxe clanked loudly as it collided with the rock. Clank! Clank! CRACK! All at once, the rock split down the middle and eight luminescent gems came clattering out across the cave floor, a few retracting after bumping into shoes. The group picked up the gems and admired them, awestruck.

"What are these?" Jericho wondered, noticeably fascinated by the rocks.

"I-I don't know. They came from that rock," JJ explained nervously, although his gaze never left the gems in his hands.

"They're beautiful," Charlotte said.

Nodding in approval to herself, Cindy said, "What she said," also transfixed on the gem's strange, vibrant beauty.

"Maybe I can find more," JJ exclaimed excitedly as he ran over and took another broad swing at the gem's origin stone.

As the pickaxe and the rock made contact, an intense beam of white light was directed into JJ's face. He fell back, grasping at his face as if it were being melted off, accidentally releasing his pickaxe, which just narrowly missed impaling Jericho's foot. The beam intensified and blasted through the ceiling, disrupting the cave's structural integrity.

"JJ!" Charlotte shrieked as she threw away her pickaxe, ran over to him, and cradled his head.

"Are you okay? Say something, anything!" She pleaded.

"Maybe a kiss will make it better," he replied, opening his eyes and smiling at her ever so slightly. Charlotte acknowledged the comment with a forced smile and a hard forehead smack.

"Oh my god!" Charlotte exclaimed, "You're burning up! You might be coming down with something."

"We're all about to be coming down with something in a minute. The cave, it *is* coming down with or without us, preferably the latter," Jericho interrupted.

Then, he pocketed two of the stones and bolted back towards the way they came. The rest of the group shared a look of agreement. JJ got to his feet, everyone pocketed two stones, snatched up their belongings, and took off after their friend. All around the group, the cave was falling away.

They were running for their lives, avoiding as much of the large falling debris as possible. They all got pegged by the occasional rock or two, but that was a small price to pay considering the alternative. They arrived at the cave mouth, and just as soon as Charlotte had stepped outside, trailing behind Cindy and Jericho, the cave mouth collapsed. When the dust and debris cleared, everyone saw that JJ was wedged under a rock from the waist down. The rock hadn't crushed him, but it was jammed well enough that he couldn't escape.

"JJ!" They all chanted in concerned unison.

"Damn, this is not my day," JJ grunted to himself as he tried to wriggle free.

They all ran over and, in turn, did every possible thing they could fathom to remove the rock. They were unsuccessful.

"UGH!" Cindy yelled, deeply frustrated by the whole situation. "Arkaine will be here any second, asking dozens of questions about what the hell's going on, and we can't even help JJ," she ranted. "And it's all because of those stupid gemstones," she said, shoving her hand in her pocket and firmly gripping a stone in her hand.

She opened it up and stared at the sandy tan colored stone. *Useless things,* she thought. *Astoundingly beautiful, but useless nonetheless.* She walked over to where JJ lay under the rock and gave another hard push. An aura of light emanated from within the hand in which Cindy held the stone. The light engulfed, at first, Cindy's hand, then her whole body. Jericho, Charlotte, and JJ all watched as Cindy's eyes rolled back. She stood this way for several moments, white-eyed and glowing. Then she blinked, and her eyes returned back to normal and the glowing ceased. Although Cindy looked as normal as ever, she had no idea how significantly, in that moment, how much her life had just severely changed.

Cindy felt a newfound strength like nothing she'd ever felt before. Her skin felt like it was buzzing, as if a constant flow of adrenaline was being pumped through her veins. She looked at everyone staring at her, and then she looked at the boulder wedged over JJ. She took four steps backward, away from the rock. She ran up towards the rock, cocked her elbows back, closed her eyes, and thrusted both of her hands straight out in front of her at the rock with all of her might. It flew ten feet easy away from where the group was standing, into the pile of rubble that was their cave. JJ went slack-jawed, then grabbed Cindy's outstretched hand and pulled himself up off the ground. He knew he was bruised, and the skin on his lower stomach stung at the slightest touch.

"How did you–" Charlotte started to ask.

"–I have no idea," Cindy said, quickly interrupting Charlotte's question.

The four stared at each other with blank expressions for a minute, pondering the mysterious episode. Then Jericho pitched a very peculiar suggestion.

"The stones. I think it was the stone," he said, reaching into his pocket.

He pulled out a large white gem. It was a rough-edged hexagon about two inches in length. The faces of it were as smooth as milk. Charlotte took a blue gem from her own pocket, close to three inches in length. It was very slender, wavy, and cold to the touch. She hadn't realized, with all the commotion, how incredibly thirsty she had become. She went into her backpack and grabbed her water bottle. She cracked it open and took a deep breath. As she raised the bottle to her lips, she saw JJ pull a bright red gem out of his pocket. She lowered the bottle and watched him intently. The gem he held was cylindrical and, if she wasn't mistaken, it seemed to have something moving inside of it. JJ just stared at it for a few seconds before it happened. He performed the same ritual that she'd seen her best friend do minutes before. He got coated in red light, and his eyes rolled back as he stood there still as a statue for seconds. Then he just blinked himself back to normal. This, whatever was happening, took a toll on him because once the light went away, JJ was down for the count.

Charlotte, who'd witnessed the whole scene, yelled Cindy's name and pointed at JJ. His head smacked the ground just before Cindy reached him. She grabbed his shoulders and started shaking him violently, pleading with him to awaken. Jericho ran over moments after Charlotte. He was hunched over and heaving to catch his breath. When Charlotte made her way over to JJ, she immediately doused JJ's face with half of her water bottle, praying he'd regain consciousness. He woke up after several seconds. Charlotte let out a sigh of relief and started drinking the rest of the water in the bottle. Just as she finished the remainder of the water, the blue stone began to glow in her hand, just as the other two gems had. Jericho stood staring and exhaling heavily beside her, and the white stone began to radiate its own light simultaneously with the blue. The pair stood petrified, as their eyes rolled back. They stood this way for a moment, then blinked and were back to normal. Soon after, Arkaine ran over and surveyed the scene. They noticed the gems in their hands had disappeared. Jericho put his hand into his pocket and pulled it out again abruptly, oblivious to the black stone that fell to the ground behind him.

"Is everybody okay?" Arkaine asked, checking the kid's faces, arms, and legs for anything major.
Arkaine was baffled that the cave had collapsed and everyone had escaped with only a few cuts and scrapes.
How could they have escaped a collapsing cave virtually unscathed? Arkaine wondered to himself.

"I got this," JJ whispered to the rest of the group. "Sir," JJ started explaining, "We were doing the assignment and we heard a very loud crack."

Arkaine rolled his eyes, clearly not impressed by the vague excuse.

"What a tremendous explanation, Rodriguez. Care to elaborate on how the hell your group managed to level a cave? No? What caused the loud crack, JJ?" Arkaine asked, snarling the question.

JJ's eyes nervously darted back and forth. Looking at each member of the group for an answer, but then, when they were all at a loss for words, he gave in.

"It was me, sir. I was messing around and caused a loud crack and collapsed the cave," JJ admitted.

"The truth. That's better. Look, is everybody okay?" Arkaine asked again.

"Yes, sir, everybody's good," JJ replied quickly.

"Good. Get your asses back to the buses, now!" Arkaine ordered.

The students complied and sulked back to the bus. All of them had the same thoughts crossing their minds as they returned to the buses. What the hell were these stones, and what had happened to them? While on the bus, the four decided to go to JJ's at 7:30 to discuss everything. They clearly had affected Cindy, but how had it affected the rest of them? And probably the most important question of all was, were they the only ones who knew about the stones, and were they going to be safe now that they'd found them?

2

A CORE TO BE CORRECT

◇ Because He's A Core Elementalist ◇

7:30 PM

Rodriguez Residence

"Has anybody made any sense of what's happened?" Jericho asked the question that everybody was thinking. "I'd like to hear everyone's ideas before I share my theory." After a few minutes of awkward silence, Jericho tried to motivate the group to give their ideas. "Your contributions could really help me conclude what's happening," he said confidently.

"All I know is that what I did earlier was freaky. But I felt powerful, and it was like the rock did what I wanted it to," Cindy explained. "In my head, I was picturing the rock as far away from JJ as possible."

"Aw," JJ said sarcastically.

Cindy silenced him with a harsh sideways glance and continued.

"In my head, I told the rock to move away. When I ran up and pushed, it did exactly that. I don't know how, but it did."

"Did everybody bring the stones?" JJ asked.

Everybody reached into their pockets to retrieve the gems. Everybody except Jericho, that is.

"No stone, Jerry?" Cindy asked him, looking confused.

"Shit, I must've dropped it at the site earlier," Jericho said quickly. "Arkaine rushed over, and I did that thing where I get nervous and put my hands in and out of my pockets. When I pulled my hand out of my pocket, that's when it probably fell. I definitely do not have it, and anybody could have picked it up after Arkaine sent us back to the bus," he finished.

"It doesn't matter anyway, for all we know it was some freak strength," JJ said, trying to convince everybody, but most of all himself. He knew something was up.

"That's not even a possibility," Cindy said, cutting down JJ's theory.

"Why would you say that?" Charlotte asked slowly.

"Because I didn't even touch the rock. I stopped like an inch short," she replied quietly.

"Are you sure?" Charlotte asked after moments of dead silence.

"How could I not be sure! I didn't touch the rock and it fucking flew! That some shit you experience and you're definitely sure you experienced it!" She screamed.

"What are these things anyway?" JJ asked aloud, quietly moving past the awkward tension.

"Those, my son, would be the Core Elementals," JJ's father answered as he descended the stairs to the basement, where the group of friends had been talking.

Cindy and Charlotte both muttered, "Uncle Anthony," and attempted to hide the stones while Jericho just sat awkwardly.

"Dad!" JJ accidentally yelled at the sudden startling surprise of his father's appearance.

"Wha-What up?" JJ asked, stuttering and trying to hastily hide the stone that he was holding as well.

"No need for the secrecy," his father said calmly. "I know all about the stones," he said, rolling up his sleeve and revealing to them the symbol that was branded into his left arm.

It was like nothing they'd ever seen before. It was beautiful, like someone had taken time to perfectly craft it so that it was art rather than a scar. It was also frightening, because nothing on this earth could've placed something so intricately there, as far as they knew. It would've looked like regular scar tissue if not for the fact that it was a dull yellow and glowed. In his other hand he held a six pointed star that had the same yellow glow as the symbol on his arm

It had a dark yellow ripple in it. Even without the vibrancy of some of the other stones, it was still quite beautiful.

"This stone, or Core to be correct, is the Lambent Core. All of the Cores we're holding contain Elemental Titans called the Core Elementals. Each Elemental can choose to bond their Life Force Energy to a host and in return the host receives Core Powers. The Elementals wait until they've found somebody with the capability to inherit, wield, control, develop, and understand these Core Powers. They are known as The Core Elementalists," he said with a dignified smile.

"Unc, how could you possibly know all of this?" Cindy asked.

"I know this because-," he started but was cut off by Jericho.

"-Because he's a Core Elementalist," Jericho finished, satisfied with himself for piecing it together.

"Correct Jericho," JJ's father said, impressed with Jericho's deductive reasoning.

"But, dad, how is that even possible?" asked JJ, questioning his father's knowledge.

"When I was twenty-two years old I was searching for new reflective material with an, ex-associate, and our search was unfruitful. One night, in a dream, I was instructed to find the Lambent Core, so I got my associate and we set out to retrieve the stone. We did. Actually *I* did. Once I bonded with the Core my associate wanted nothing to do with me, so we parted ways. Within forty-eight hours I was, well, per lack of a better term, branded with my Core Symbol. The Symbol and the Core are made of the same thing. When I first bonded with the Lambent Core I thought I'd lost it. Not mentally, literally. I searched for days on end but it was nowhere to be found. Two days later, I was plagued with pain from the Symbol's branding and once it was over the stone was back in my hand."
Everyone was a bit shocked by Mr. Rodriguez's story even though the proof really was overwhelming. Jericho cleared his throat and spoke.

"That's all really amazing Pops but I gotta ask you a question."

"Shoot."

"How, in the entirety of the universe, can any of this be remotely possible?"

"Well everybody, this is pretty much the extent of what I know about the Elementals and the Cores," he began, seating himself in a comfy lounge chair in the middle of the room.

His eyes exploded with a fierce yellow light. A massive flowing aura of blazing yellow energy radiated from his body. The four of them could do nothing but stare in awe. Mr. Rodriguez's power was truly amazing, unlike anything any of them had ever seen. He cupped both of his hands on his lap and formed a circle with his fingers, stretching them as wide as they could go. He closed his eyes and as soon as his eyelids sealed, all of the light in the room disappeared. Every lamp, every TV, and every console was completely devoid of light. Even the aura had completely vanished. JJ's dad sat perfectly still in the darkness. The only sound he made were the faintest exhales. Jericho slowly counted each moment they spent in the dark inside his head.
One. Two. Three. Fo-

Mr. Rodriguez's yellow eyes blazed to life and a giant dark blue aurora of lights encompassed the entirety of the area directly in front of him.

"A long time ago, eons before our world even existed, there was only one thing in existence: The Core Being. It created the Core Planet, for which all of the Core Elementals, giant beings made of pure elemental energy, were made," he continued.

As he spoke the lights swirled around changing their color and shape to illustrate the story as he narrated.

"The Core Being created the Elementals by removing a piece of itself and infusing its Life Force Energy into it to transform it into an Elemental. The Core Planet's sole purpose was to contain and sustain all of the Core Elementals.

In the beginning, four Elementals were created; Earth, the foundation amongst the Elementals, Strong and bold. Water, the peace amongst the Elementals, Healing and nurturing. Air, the intelligence amongst the Elementals, Wise and understanding. Fire, the heart amongst the Elementals, Courageous and headstrong. After some centuries of sculpting the planet, the Elementals grew tired of the repetitive routine. The Core Being took notice and allowed the Elementals to connect and evolve. New Elementals were created over time by the Elementals and the Core Being. Lava, Plant, Ice, Thunder, and Lightning, all were new evolutions and Elementals that were created. Each and every Elemental was created with an equal and opposite counter. Fire with Water, Earth with Air, Thunder with Lightning, Lava with Ice, and so forth.

After many millennia, countless evolutions had been made and the Core Planet was a beautiful system of Elementals. With so many Elementals roaming the confines of the planet, brawls would break out between them over territories and dominance, causing mass amounts of destruction. The Core Being understood that balance needed to be kept because if the disturbance and instability continued, the Elementals could wage war against one another and destroy the whole planet. The Core Being had no choice but to make an Elemental powerful enough to handle such a burden. The Core Being commenced to make its greatest Elemental. It had created the purest Core Elemental to ever exist, Light. Although it had created such a beautiful and pure Elemental, it had to create a Core Elemental that could be the perfect counter. It had to create something very dark and most impure. It had to create, Chaos.

The Chaos Elemental was evil, disfigured, and malicious. Chaos knew no limits and grew rapidly. It began taking over other Elementals, consuming and controlling their power whilst destroying everything in Its path. Chaos gathered together the Elementals before turning them against the Core Being. Eventually, it mustered the strength and audacity to coordinate an attack on the Core Being, using its combined power that it had parasitically acquired from the other Elementals. Then the Core Being, Maker of All The Elementals, began fighting back Chaos' revolution using Light. Using its own Life Force Energy, It gave Light the power to amass and influence other Elementals to rebel against Chaos. Light became the Core Being's disciple, absorbing the Core Being's energy to fight against Chaos's uprising. Light and Chaos waged war against one another, each of them leading an army and struggling to gain absolute control over the Elementals. Chaos was stunned at Light's newfound power and understood the only way for Light to have achieved such power is if the Core Being had enhanced Light by infusing Its own Life Force Energy into It. Chaos seized the opportunity to prey on the Core Being's vulnerability and launched a massive attack, using the powers of all of the Elementals it still had control over. The full on attack was so powerful that it disrupted the Core Being's internal balance. It began to crack in many places releasing many different colored beams of light in every direction. The Core Being broke apart in the massive explosion, pieces of the Core Being flying everywhere-."

"Excuse me," Cindy interjected, "Was that The Big Bang?" she asked.

Mr. Rodriguez gave her a wink, and nodded yes. Then he continued.

"As the dull and colorless shards of the Core Being lay around, Elementals started losing their stability, and their

Life Force Energy started getting sucked into the shards and becoming trapped inside. Chaos, believing that It had successfully brought the downfall of the Core Planet, commenced taking control of Elementals and spreading destruction. As Chaos was destroying the Core Planet, It came across a crater littered with shards of the Core Being. As one final act of spite towards Its creator, Chaos raised a massive foot to stomp on them. When Its foot touched down some of Its Chaotic Energy became trapped in the shards. Chaos' power started diminishing and the Elementals that It was controlling were being freed from Its parasitic grasp. It grabbed up the shards from where they lay and, too late, discovered this was a grave mistake. Chaos' Life Force Energy was sucked into three separate Core Being pieces, which then conjoined into a single shard of raw Chaotic energy. Chaos was caged in the shards, no longer an Elemental Titan capable of influencing nature, this was now an Elemental Core. Chaos was imprisoned and compressed into a concentrated ingot of pure Elemental energy and had been transformed into the Mayhem Core. Now that Chaos had been contained as the Mayhem Core it no longer had the ability to control other Elementals. Light was victorious and peace was restored.

Light went on to restore the Core Planet back to its original design with ease, returning borrowed power, when all of a sudden, Its own power began to dwindle. Light's power waned until six Core Being shards inhaled the Life Force Energy of Light. Light too had become a concentrated ingot of pure Elemental energy, the Lambent Core, when the six

Light shards fused together. In turn, all of the Elementals were transformed into ingots of untamed Elemental energy. Each with the potential to fight with Light or for Chaos to one day restore the Core Planet back to its former glory. I believe this is the reason the Core Elementalists exist and why they're so important. To be the vessels in which the battle shall continue. As far as I know countless Core Elementals exist, but I've only accounted for our seven. As for Core Elementalists, I am the last no longer. You four will become the new Elementalists. I'll do my best to explain the full extent of my powers and help you to learn about and develop your own. In time. But first, there is something you need to know."

The aurora dissipated and the room lit back up.

"Your dad is wicked," Cindy said to JJ. "Without a doubt, I believe every word."

"Wait," squealed Charlotte. "You said *our seven* towards the end. Ours who? I mean yours and who else's? There are other people who know about the Cores?" She asked.

"Yes there are others. We were strangers when we all first met. They were the original Core Elementalists and my best friends. They were actually," he paused for several seconds then sighed deeply, "they were actually," he repeated again.

He stared up at the ceiling quietly while the other four stared at him in quiet anticipation.

When he finally spoke he said, "They were your parents. Me, Natasha, Sylvia, and Oliver," he told them.

"That's only five," Jericho told him.

"Well the other two, you've never met. There was a woman who possessed Fire and a man who possessed Shadow. There was a woman who used to wield Chaos, but nobody ever met her except the woman who had Fire. As far as I know, we're the only ones who know anything about the Cores," he finished. "Oh, and Arthur," he added quickly, saying the name with a hint of disgust, but his eyes seemed to withhold a sadness he didn't share.

"Our parents," Charlotte repeated skeptically, "Our parents were superheroes? Sorry Uncle Anthony, I just don't buy that my dad was ever super at-," she was saying before Jericho cut her off.

"-Shut up! Shut up! You said Arthur right?" Jericho asked Mr. Rodriguez.

"I did," he replied.

"Okay because I clearly wasn't just talking," Charlotte said loudly.

"We'll come back to that," Jericho said to her. "Back to what I was saying to you. Unc, this Arthur guy, his last name wouldn't happen to be Arkaine, would it?"

Mr. Rodriguez's eyes widened into saucers.

"How did you know that?" He asked quickly, a touch of fear residing in the question.

Jericho and his friends passed a wary look between them. His gaze landed back on JJ's dad.

"Arthur Arkaine is one of our teachers. He's the one who took us on the field trip where we found all of the Cores," he told him.

"It's probably not a coincidence. He's been searching for one ever since he saw me bond with the Lambent Core," JJ's dad said.

"Whoa!" Cindy said loudly. "Arkaine was your, quote unquote, ex-associate? That's unbeli-. Actually that kinda makes a helluva lot of sense."

Mr. Rodriguez looked down at the floor and thought over everything they'd been discussing.

"You have all the Cores you found, right?" He asked everyone but stared directly at JJ.

"Not exactly," JJ said quietly.

"What do you mean Justin?"

JJ replied, "I mean, some of them are gone dad. I guess we lost them."

"Are you sure you lost them and didn't bond with them instead?"

"How exactly would we know if we bonded with them?" Jericho asked.

"Well, the Core would illuminate your body and your eyes would whiten as the Elemental fuses Its energy to your DNA. Then they would vanish. Trust me, you'd know. This absolutely has not happened yet, right?" Mr. Rodriguez answered and asked carefully.

The four looked at each other in silence for almost a minute before JJ worked up the nerve to speak.

"Right?" He repeated.

"Dad," he spoke nervously, "I think that happened to all of us."

His dad's face hardened and with a stern voice he commanded, "Take out the Cores and tell me what happened, now!"

3

I'M NOT A SUPERHERO

◇ It Sounds More Like Possession ◇

9:45 PM

Rodriguez Residence

They all took the Cores from where they'd attempted to hide them at. Mr. Rodriguez stared at the Cores and was still amazed at their beauty. No matter how many Cores you see you realize that none of them look the same and they're all stunningly beautiful. He watched how the Cores glowed slightly brighter than his own, meaning they were unclaimed. In his son's outstretched hand was a bright orange hemisphere with a deep black spiral continually swirling within it. In Cindy's hand was a short and stretched bright green triangular prism that had a network of dark green spider-webbed veins stretching across its surface. Charlotte held out her hand and showed him a rhombus as clear as glass that was freckled with bright periwinkle dots. As he stared at the transparent shape, he noticed that the dots would fade and reappear.

"Talk," Mr. Rodriguez said as he rolled over a computer chair and sat down in front of the group.

JJ started telling him the story about what happened while they were down in the caves. When he got to the part about the cave mouth collapsing around him, his dad shifted uncomfortably in his seat.

"So then I was just lying there after they all tried to move it and I was just trapped. I couldn't wriggle free no matter what I tried then," JJ's voice trailed off.

"Then what?" His dad asked.

"Cindy. She had a, moment, then pushed the rock, I guess."

Mr. Rodriguez turned and focused his attention onto Cindy.

"Cinthya," he said softly. "I hear you had a moment. Tell me about it," he requested.

Quietly, Cindy spoke, "Okay this is what happened. I was yelling because Arkaine was coming and JJ was trapped under a rock. I had an adrenaline rush but it felt like, stronger than a normal one, I guess. I don't know. Anyway, after the rush I ran up to the rock and pushed it away."

Mr. Rodriguez gently asked, "How far?"

Cindy bit her lip nervously. "Like nine or ten feet maybe."

"So, you pushed a rock ten feet off of and away from JJ and he didn't get hurt," he restated.

"Right except, I didn't actually push the rock. I pushed, at, the rock, and it sort of flew away from him. It was strange."

"Did you have a Core in your hands before the alleged adrenaline rush?"

"Yeah. A sandy oval one with pointy edges."

"Sounds like you bonded with the Terra Core. It contains the Earth Elemental."

Tell them, said the voice in Mr. Rodriguez's head.

"Are you sure now's the right time? We're not even a hundred percent sure about what Cores they've bonded with. Also, we were supposed to attempt this in a regulated environment. Also, also, their parents were supposed to be here for all of this, if you can recall," Mr. Rodriguez said aloud to the voice in his head.

Yes. They need to know, the voice said.

"Dad, who are you talking to?" JJ asked.

"There's something that I need to tell you all that is really important," his dad said.

"Which is?"

"Well? It's a sort of a *side effect* to all of this great power."

Cindy exhaled deeply and wiped her face dramatically.

"Of course there's a catch," she said. "There's always a freaking catch. What is it?"

"There's no exact definition but if I had to give it an official title, I'd call it, schizophrenia."

"Wow," Charlotte said loudly. "So we're all going to be psychos?" She asked, unable to hide the concern in her voice.

"No. You will just have an Elemental inhabiting your mind and body," Mr. Rodriguez replied.

"It sounds more like possession than schizophrenia," Jericho noted. "I don't like the idea of a poltergeist."

"Look," Mr. Rodriguez said fiercely, "it's a trade-off. The Elementals get to exist using the Elementalist as a vessel and the Elementalists get to wield the Elemental's energy."

"Oh wait," JJ said, "that actually sounds like a fair trade. And they're good right, like, they won't kill us?"

"No, they will not kill you and yes, they are good."
"Yup. Win, win to me."

Cindy slammed her hands on her thighs and smiled.

"I agree with JJ," she told everyone.

"Me too," Jericho agreed.

"Not really much of a choice. *I already bonded.* And if all of you are in, I'm obviously in. God knows you can't take care of yourselves," Charlotte joked.

"So," Mr. Rodriguez said to get everyone's attention, "you want to meet Light?"

"Yeah! Wait, what?" JJ asked confused, realizing he'd gotten too excited and didn't really listen to the question before answering.

"My Elemental, Light. Want to meet him? Ask him questions, that sort of thing?"

The group stared at one another with slightly confused looks.

"So you mean we can, like, talk to Light?" Cindy asked.

"Yes," Jericho said quickly. "He literally just said that."

"Holy freaking crap, could you be more of a pain in the a-," she started to snap when she realized what JJ's dad was doing.

Mr. Rodriguez's eyes began to glow a burning yellow and a matching yellow aura swelled around him. When he spoke to them, the voice that crossed his lips wasn't his own.

"Hello Elementalists, I am the Light Elemental, but it would probably be more comfortable if you just called me Light," Light told them.

"Uh, hi, I-I'm Justin Joseph, but you can call me JJ," JJ told Light.

"There's actually no need for introductions because I share all of Anthony's thoughts so I know you all as well as he does," Light explained.

"Oh, well then, uh," JJ trailed off into an awkward silence.

Let them introduce themselves, Anthony said to Light inside his mind.

Why? Light asked.

Really? You're going to make me explain?

Mr. Rodriguez waited for Light to answer back, but it didn't.

It will put them at ease and relieve the tension, he explained.

Alright, I'll do it.

"Anthony tells me that introducing yourselves will put you more at ease so," Light stopped talking and pointed at Jericho, "you introduce yourself please."

Jericho exhaled deeply and said, "I'm Jericho and," he pointed to Charlotte.

"I'm Charlotte," she said nervously.

"I'm Cindy," she introduced herself.

"Excellent," Light said excitedly. "Do you feel any better?"

"Actually, I kind of do," JJ said.

"Anthony has always been good with people," Light told them. "Now, do you have any questions for me?"

At first no one said a word, too nervous to be the first one to speak up.

"I do," Cindy said, finally shattering the silence, "but it's not for you. It's for Uncle Ant."

"Get on then, he can hear you. Ask your question," Light said encouragingly.

Cindy cleared her throat loudly and asked her question. "Does this," she paused to find the right word, "*unification* hurt you at all?"

While his eyes still glowed, JJ's dad spoke.

"No, not at all," he told her. "It feels warm and fuzzy more than anything, like hot cocoa warming a cold body with the intensity of a star."

"Alright," Cindy said, sounding satisfied with the response. "Doesn't sound that bad at all. Kinda cool actually."

Mr. Rodriguez's voice changed back into Light's.

"So you've bonded with the Terra Core?" Light asked Cindy.

"Supposedly," she answered.

"If I had to guess I would say that Anthony's assumption is probably correct. You are a spitting image of Ms. Sylvia except your hair is far more interesting."

Cindy started blushing and an uncontainable smile stretched across her lips.

"You seem worthy to be Earth's new Elementalist," Light declared.

"Thank you Light," Cindy said appreciatively. "What's the Earth Elemental like?"
"Well," Light started, "Earth is grounded, no pun intended. Very-."

"-Come on," JJ interrupted. "You clearly intended that pun," he called him out.

Light smiled at him and started to laugh a simple calm chuckle.

"You got me," Light confessed. "Anyway, Earth is very helpful and strong. One of the strongest amongst the Four. Also, Earth is very kind, caring, and thoughtful."

"Wow. I didn't think I'd ever be this excited to be skitzo," Cindy said and chuckled to herself.

Mr. Rodriguez's eyes stopped glowing.

"So I suppose we should try to guess what Elementals bonded with the rest of you," he said to everyone.

JJ cut in, "The Core I bonded with was red and was like, a cylinder dad. Do you know which one it was?"

Sounds like Fire, Light said in Mr. Rodriguez's head.

Exactly what I was thinking, Mr. Rodriguez said back.

I know.

Funny. Your sense of humor is getting better.

Almost three decades I've been in your head Anthony, I was bound to adopt some sort of comedic stance.

I suppose.

"Light and I believe that was the Fire Elemental's Pyro Core. That's going to be an interesting fit," JJ's dad told his son.

It will, quite literally, be a hot mess Anthony, Light joked.

I couldn't agree more, but it will be interesting nonetheless, he said back to Light.

"We'll know for sure when you get your Core Symbol," he said. "Jericho, what did yours look like?"

"It was white and smooth. I don't remember what shape it was, though," Jericho responded.

What do you think? Mr. Rodriguez asked Light.

I think the Four were found together, after all, that is Miss Umpter's son if I'm not mistaken. They spent over a decade together on this planet with Elementalists before being caged again. It seems fitting they'd do what they could to stay together whilst imprisoned, Light explained.

"That wasn't very well detailed but if the Terra Core and the Pyro Core were found in the same place, we assume the Four were together, and you also found the Turbulent Core and the Aquarius Core," Mr. Rodriguez said.

"Then I'm assuming that the blue Core I found was the Aquarius Core," Charlotte said.

"Probably but like I said to JJ, you'll need to get your Symbols to be sure."

"Okay, but you said we'd get Core Powers and that you have Core Powers, right?" Cindy asked.

"That's right," Mr. Rodriguez confirmed.

"So when exactly will that be?" Charlotte asked him.

"Well, shortly after you get your Symbols you all will become extreme elemental powerhouses," he replied.

Jericho chimed in and asked, "When you say powerhouses you mean what exactly?"

"Well, the Elemental's energy is incredibly powerful and when you get your Symbol that means their Life Force Energy is finished bonding with your DNA. Once that happens you'll need to develop a connection with the Elemental. This usually happens better if you can create a strong emotional connection so they can latch themselves to your mind," Mr. Rodriguez finished explaining.

"Hence, the schizophrenia," Jericho noted.

"Exactly. Also," Mr. Rodriguez added, "you'll probably burn something," he pointed at JJ, "Soak something," he pointed at Charlotte, "Blow something away," he pointed at Jericho, "And destroy something," he finished and pointed at Cindy.

"That is if we're even correct about what Cores you've bonded with. Not to mention the physical enhancements that come with the bonding process."

"Enhancements?" Charlotte echoed as a question, curiosity suddenly peaked.

"Yes it's another side effect of the unification, as Cindy put it, but this is a positive effect. All of your senses will become heightened. Your body's natural ability to heal will increase tenfold. That doesn't mean you're indestructible though, I can't stress this enough," he explained, casting a stern and cautionary warning glance at everyone. "Also by sharing your mind with an Elemental you gain access to an immense amount of memory and knowledge. They never forget a single thing," he continued as they listened intently. "Everything that you can see, they can see. Everything that you're taught, they learn as well and they remember every single thing in perfect detail. You will learn just how powerful of an ability this is but we can leave it there for now. Your muscle mass will practically double overnight and your strength will increase as well. Then there's your speed. Charlotte will probably be the fastest of you due to her experience winning in cross country but all of you will see a dramatic increase in your running speed. You'll be much more nimble than before and your overall physicality will shift to make you faster, stronger, and sharper. All of this is needed to become a fully realized Elementalist."

Charlotte thought it all over then offered up a question.

"Does having a different Elemental have an effect on your physical enhancements?" She asked.

"No," he answered, still mulling it over. "That is determined by your own physical condition. The only thing that would differ is your Elemental itself. They tend to take on the personality of their Elementalist so from person to person they may talk and act differently but until you get your Symbol, we can't even truly be sure what Elemental you've even bonded with. The only way to even be kind of sure would be to use your Core Powers in some sort of premature way, like what you all explained happened to Ms. Thompson earlier today."

"Okay, so is that a good thing or a bad thing?" Cindy asked.

Neither good nor bad, Light said in Mr. Rodriguez's mind. *It probably just means she'll be really powerful, like you.*

"I honestly wouldn't classify it as neither good nor bad. I'd say it's more unprecedented than anything else," he told her.

"Great. So now if you don't mind I would love to back track," Charlotte said, "And talk about the fact that you said our parents were Core Elementalists."

Mr. Rodriguez checked his watch and the time read 22:50.

"It's getting late and you all have school tomorrow. Come straight here after and I'll tell you what you want to know," he told them. "Upstairs, come on. Let's go."

Cindy, Charlotte, and Jericho trudged up the stairs followed by JJ and his father. They got into their cars and turned on the engines.

"Night pops," Jericho called.

"Night Jericho," he called back. "Night girls, drive safe," he called to the girls.

After they both replied, "We will, night guys." JJ yelled to everyone, "Text me when you get home!"

They began pulling away and JJ and his dad walked back into their house and both took a seat in the living room. Mr. Rodriguez looked at his son sitting on the couch across the room uncharacteristically quiet.

"You okay kid?" He asked JJ.

"I mean, yeah. All of that was just," he paused then mimicked an explosion by his head with his hands. "It was a lot. I don't know what to think right now."

"What do you mean? You don't know what to think about what?"

"Dad," he said, "You are the CEO of a solar panel company. You're forty-seven with doctorates in physics, geology, mechanics and bio-mechanics, literature, economics, business and business management, computer science, astronomy, and astrology. To say you're overqualified for *everything* would be an understatement. Damn, I am just now realizing why you have all these freaking degrees. 'Cause now, all of a sudden, you're a retired superhero? Please, tell me what I'm supposed to think."

"First, I'm not retired. I'm more like, on reserve. Second, I'm not a superhero-," he said before JJ interrupted.

"-then explain to me what just happened in the basement!" JJ shouted.

"If you'll let me finish my sentence. I was saying, I'm not a superhero, I'm an Elementalist. Some people are incredibly smart or incredibly strong, but-," was all he could say before JJ interrupted again.

"-but you dad. You manipulate light like a magical projector and try to compare that to a bodybuilder lifting a thousand pounds. But I guess it's just apples to oranges, huh?"

"I mean I wouldn't say its apples to oranges, more like a gifted human to a regular human but-."

"-you have an Elemental space titan living in your head."

"Call it a mild case of schizophrenia."

"That's not a valid justification!"

He's right, Light said.

Who's side are you on? Mr. Rodriguez asked, feeling somewhat offended.

Yours, Light confirmed, *but when he's right, he's right.*

Shut up.

Rude.

"That's all I got," his dad told him.

"It's not good enough," JJ snapped back.

"I'm sorry," he apologized.

"You can manipulate light like it's an everyday object," he stated, his expression and tone both cold and enigmatic.

"Amongst other things."

"Amongst other things," he repeated in disbelief. "I'm going to bed dad, I have a headache. This is just too much to process in a night."

"That's a good idea, you have school in the morning."

"Yup."

"Good night. I love you JJ."

"Love you too dad. Will you be here when I get home tomorrow?"

"As far as I know."

"Cool. G'night."

4

THAT WAS SOME OTHERWORLDLY TYPE SHIT

◇ Old Friends, New Beginnings ◇

Arthur Malum Arkaine
Anthony James Rodriguez
25 Years Ago

"Anthony, what're we doing here? Why are we in the caves looking for this lamping corn you saw in a dream?" Arthur asked his best friend Anthony.

"That's Lambent Core, Art," Anthony replied.

"It's special, I know it, Arthur. How else do you explain a dream so vivid and specific that it told me exactly where to find this Lambent Core down to the cave and rock formation?" He questioned Arthur as he continued to strike the rock exactly where he'd seen it in his dream.

"Anthony," Arthur said, getting his friend's attention, "I'd do anything for you," he said.

"I know Art," Anthony said back, acknowledging the sincerity in his friend's voice.

"What do you think you're gonna do with this Core once you find it?"

"I know exactly what to do when the time comes. Trust me," he said reassuringly.

Anthony patted his backpack with the items he saw in his dream. He had a bag of cotton balls and matches so he could make a fire and a heavy duty portable flashlight. When he found the Core, he'd ignite the fire and illuminate the flashlight then something amazing would happen. The voice he'd heard in his dream said that it was gonna be life changing and he couldn't wait. Anthony worked steadily without rest and showed no sign of slowing even after hours of labor. He continually performed the tedious task of striking the same area over and over. Anthony knew that with each strike he was getting closer to his goal and in the end the reward would be incomparable. After six hours it finally happened. He saw a bright yellow glow from the rock as a huge chunk fell away.

"This is it!" Anthony exclaimed.

Arthur looked at the stone in his friend's hand and couldn't believe his own eyes. Anthony was holding the very thing he had described to him at 2:30 AM that very morning, right after he'd had the dream. The Lambent Core. Its beauty was unmatched by anything Arthur had ever seen in person, in a picture, or in a dream. Arthur was amazed that his friend had somehow had this prophetic dream where he uncovered the exact location of the beauteous stone.

"Arthur, please understand that what I'm gonna do next is probably going to seem scary and somewhat unreal but, I saw it in a dream after all," he explained slowly.

"Okay dude, you're being really creepy. Just do what you gotta do and I'm gonna wait outside. This cave gives me the creeps, even more than you do," Arthur joked, nudging Anthony with his elbow.

As Arthur walked away, Anthony began performing the ritual he'd seen. He unzipped his backpack and grabbed all of his supplies. He squatted down and opened the plastic bag full of cotton balls. Then he struck a match and ignited every match on the pad before dropping it into the middle of the white cotton fluff. As the fire blazed he put in his backpack which also ignited after a few moments of waiting. He fiddled with the medallion around his neck which was inscribed with the names 'Justin and Joseph', his younger twin brothers who died in a car crash when they were eleven. He was only thirteen then and that was almost nine years ago. His best friend, Arthur, was with him through it all and

Anthony would never forget the debt he owed him for being there for him, even though his home was becoming broken. Arthur was a true friend.

Anthony picked up the portable flashlight, switched it on, and placed it upright on the floor. He stared at the crackling fire and waited for it to reach its pinnacle before reaching into his pants pocket and grabbing the six pointed star shaped stone. He clasped the stone within both of his hands. He knelt down and within moments he was swallowed by a blazing light and his eyes rolled back into his head. He stood frozen in place for minutes. From outside the cave, Arthur saw the light spilling out and decided to peek in on his best friend, just in case.

When Arthur saw what was going on inside, he couldn't believe his eyes. Anthony was glowing, literally glowing. He was surrounded by a deep yellow aura of light that pulsated around him and his eyes were even stranger than the light. They were milky white and lifeless. He crept cautiously into the cave and got closer to his friend. As if all that was occurring weren't intense enough, about thirty seconds into his creep toward Anthony, another bizarre feat occurred. The fire light and flashlight glow intensified beyond belief and shot into the middle of Anthony's chest, fusing into a conjoined beam along the way. For seconds, Anthony stood paralyzed absorbing the blast before the cave was blanketed by complete darkness and silence. Anthony opened his eyes and saw nothing but could hear his friend's breathing.

"Arthur," he spoke into the darkness.

"Yes," came Arthur's reply after several seconds.

"You okay?"

"Me? I'm perfectly fine but. A-are you okay?" he asked, unable to contain the worry in his voice.

"I'm good," he assured. "Wish I could see though," he said, closing and rubbing his eyes vigorously.

"Me too," said Arthur in agreement.

Anthony opened his eyes and to his amazement, he could see perfectly. *This wasn't in the dream*, he thought to himself. He looked around and saw Arthur feeling the wall looking confused.

"Arthur. Follow me," Anthony instructed.

Anthony took Arthur's hand and guided his friend safely out of the pitch black cave into the cover of night. Arthur was baffled that Anthony had so expertly maneuvered out of the cave in the dark, when he was lost as a dog. Was it some part of his futuristic dream vision thing? Or did it have something to do with the crazy beam of light he'd witnessed strike him while in the cave?

If you want answers Arthur, then you need to speak up and ask, he said to himself.

"Anthony," Arthur said, getting his friend's attention, "How'd you know *exactly* how to get out of that cave through the dark? I mean, I couldn't tell which way was up but you grabbed my hand and led me straight out. How?"

"Honestly Art, I can see in the dark with no problem," he said it as if it were the most normal thing he'd ever said. "In my dream, somebody told me that I'd get abilities and the Lambent Core is the reason," he explained while searching his pockets for the Core. "I can't find it Art!"

"Ant, calm down."

"I'm going back in to find it!" he said, ignoring his friend, turning, and running back towards the cave.

Anthony came out of the cave twenty minutes later looking disappointed.

"You didn't find it, I'm guessing," Arthur said.

"What was your first clue, Sherlock?" Anthony asked rhetorically.

"Well your face looks sad as hell, if I'm being honest."

Anthony walked past his friend towards the Jeep, his gaze never leaving the ground. Arthur followed behind him quietly before a thought popped into his head.

"Wait, wait, wait," he said to Anthony's back.

"What?"

"You have powers now?"

"Yeah, I guess so," he said, picking his head up and actually processing that information. He turned around, grabbed his friend's shoulders, and said loudly, "I have powers Art! I have powers!"

Arthur pushed him off and said, "Good for you. Don't rub it in."

"What's the matter? Are you really acting jealous right now?"

"No Ant. Of course I'm not jealous that my best friend got powers from a magic dream rock and then lost it."

"I can't believe this. Okay, yeah I've got powers and I don't know where the Lambent Core is but how can you be so stupid Art?"

"Oh! So now, I'm stupid?"

"If I have powers Arthur and you don't, then you should automatically know that *we* have powers. Just like if *you* had powers and I didn't. *Lo mío es tuyo, lo tuyo es mío.* Or did somehow me finding that Core result in you forgetting that."

"Please spare me the lecture on how we're brothers Anthony. If what's yours was mine then you wouldn't have lost the Core and we could both be standing here with powers."

"You're being really childish right now. I need you to grow a pair and get over yourself."

"What makes you so special Anthony?"

He was taken aback by the question and the insinuation.

"What makes me so-," he started to repeat.

"-What are you asking me right now?"

"What makes you so damn special?" Arthur yelled, an unquenchable bitterness climbing up his throat.

"Nothing. I don't. Arthur," he stammered.

"You aren't more important than me! You aren't better than me! I saw what happened in that cave and I have got to say that was some otherworldly type shit. You should be dead Anthony, or at the very least burned or something. You got hit with fire. You got powers. I get," his voice trailed off.

"Nothing," Anthony whispered, "Oh Art."

"Nothing!" Arthur screamed and fell to his knees as tears started down his face.

Anthony reached down and touched Arthur's shoulder. Arthur pulled away and looked up at Anthony. He stood up and wiped his tears away with the bottom of his shirt.

"What's yours is mine right?" Arthur asked in a shaky voice.

A quiet, "Arthur," was all Anthony could manage.

Through clenched teeth Arthur repeated, "What's yours is mine right?"

Anthony sighed. "Of course."

"Then share your powers with me."

Anthony shook his head in confusion, sadness, and disbelief.

"Arthur, you're my best friend. Don't do this."

"Share your damn powers, Anthony."

"I, uh, I," Anthony stuttered.

"Typical. So that's a no?"

"I can't Arthur. You know that."

A mask of fury washed over Arthur's face and his skin turned a burning shade of red.

"I don't know a fucking thing about these powers you claim to have!" Arthur screamed directly in his best friend's face. "I don't know a fucking thing about what really happened in that cave! And apparently, I don't know a fucking thing about you!"

A lonely tear streamed down Anthony's cheek.

"You know me Arthur," he whimpered. "We're best friends. Calm down, this isn't like you."

Arthur let out an obviously fake laugh.

"That's rich. You're telling me what to do because now that you found that stupid stone you're gonna be so goddamn important. What gives you the right to tell me what to do? Nothing," Arthur said walking towards Anthony with his fists clenched.

When he was close enough to Anthony, he swung on him. Anthony dodged the punch with ease and Arthur threw four more punches. Anthony dodged every blow and pushed Arthur to the ground.

"I won't fight you Arthur. You're like a brother to me," Anthony said to him, trying hopefully to snap him out of his rage. It was no use.

Arthur spit a fat loogie at him. "You're dead to me Anthony. You are clearly too important to hang around with regular people like me," Arthur snapped, the spite in his voice crystal clear.

"Don't be like this Art," Anthony pleaded.

"Fuck off," Arthur said as he got up and walked away.

After that the two of them parted ways and never saw or heard from one another. Anthony continued to have dreams with the voice guiding him to do things that he'd never imagined were possible. It instructed him to further the development of his abilities and to push the limits of his mind. It showed him images of people with Cores, some who had come together to form a small group.

Months had passed and the dream voice, who he now knew was the Elemental space titan known as Light, told Anthony that he would have to protect the Cores with his life and when the time comes he may have to risk everything to save the universe. Anthony overcame his unwillingness to accept his fate and vowed to keep Cores and Core Elementalists alive, wherever they might show up. Arthur however had other plans. He became obsessed with finding Cores of his own and dedicated his life to searching the caves where

Anthony had found his. He may not have had an omniscient dream instructor but his incessant need to prove he was just as important as Anthony drove him to the conclusion that by controlling the Cores and commanding a super powered army, he could do whatever he wanted, whenever he wanted, answering to no one but himself. Only then would he truly be more important than Anthony ever could.

Anthony met up with the five other Core Elementalists. The six of them banded together and kept defeating Chaos' beasts in areas where they grew numerously and terrorized the world unguided without a Chaos Elementalist. Throughout their travels they came across an evil Core Elementalist named Grey Shadow, who could loosely control the beasts and manipulate shadows. They continued to fight against him and the shadow beasts. They forcefully defeated Grey Shadow and learned that his Elemental was a direct descendant of Chaos and was doomed to be corrupted. Eventually they converted him into a semi-trustworthy ally but he retreated back to his village and vowed to clear his life of chaotic corruption. Anthony and his group of allies continued fending off the shadow beasts while also pursuing their own personal lives, until the time arose when they wanted to start the next phase.

Arthur's quest however, was without success until the day of his twelfth annual cave exploration excavation field trip. He'd been teaching for twelve years at West San Diego High School and each year, towards the end of the year, he took his students to the caves where Anthony had found the

Lambent Core. Once there he made them dig further and further into the caves in hopes that one day one of the students would find a Core. After a long unsuccessful search, students had uncovered Cores or at the very least *one* Core. As he was chastising a group of students who'd miraculously survived a cave folding in on itself, he noticed a black stone on the ground behind their feet. Arthur instantly knew that the stone was definitely a Core.

Now as far as Arthur knew, Cores were just something somebody once saw in a dream but he had a good feeling about this. Whatever Anthony had found that night, this was something like it, but completely different. This Core had a different energy than the one he'd seen before and very distinctive features. First, it was a very deep black and it didn't glow so much as it radiated darkness. It also had a rugged formation, as if multiple pieces had been put under intense pressure and morphed together. Arthur held the Core in his hands and was overcome with an overwhelming sense of malice, which he sort of liked in a strange way. It felt empowering.

Arthur stood in front of the coach bus and stared angrily at the caves. Almost twenty-one years and all he had to show for it was one Core. A new found rage suddenly boiled up inside of Arthur. He reached into his bag and felt around to make sure the time charges were still there and inactive. Then he went from cave to cave dismissing students back to the bus, placing and activating the bomb timers just before leaving. Twenty-four hours and the caves would be blown to rubble. He'd be back in time to make sure that everything went accordingly.

"These caves are worthless," Arthur thought aloud. "So let 'em blow," he said slowly with a sinister smile stretching across his lips.

5

WELL LET'S START A NEW CHAPTER

◇ What's A Core? ◇

10:15 AM
Dr. Arkaine's Archaeology Class

JJ gulped. He was a gazelle who had accidentally staggered into a den of waking lions. Arkaine was picking on him and his friends, he knew, because he wanted to see how they'd react. If there was one thing JJ could do, it was handle intense situations by staying calm under pressure.

Charlotte, Cindy, JJ, and Jericho walked to the front of the class. They all had their post-dig homework papers and took turns reading.

"We found many samples of sedimentary rock such as limestone and calcite," Cindy read aloud.

"The cave was also damp and humid," JJ added.

"There was little to no life found inside the cave," Jericho yawned. "Excuse me," he said.

"Pardoned," Arkaine grumbled, "Continue."

"I didn't know if I should've put down this observation or not," Charlotte said addressing the class and Arkaine, "But our cave collapsed around us."

The four of them took turns reading boring observations. After fifteen minutes, they'd finished presenting.

"Before you take a seat I have a final question. Did you find anything of interest in the cave before it miraculously collapsed around you all?" Arkaine asked, suppressing a smile.

Of course all of them understood the question that he was really asking them. *Did you find any Cores that I should know about?* JJ would usually act impetuously and say something to fix everything but that wasn't the case this time. For one of the few times in his life, JJ was completely tongue tied. The group waited for JJ to help the situation with the Gift of Gab, but it never came. Jericho took it upon himself to take over JJ's spot as the speaker of the group.

"No sir. Just your average sedimentary formations like Cindy said. It was dark and we were working by the lights on our helmets, then the cave started to collapse," Jericho explained. "We barely managed to get ourselves out in one piece. So to answer your question again, no. Nothing of too much interest," he finished.

"Thank you for that unnecessarily long explanation. A simple *no* would have sufficed, Mr. Umpter," Arkaine said harshly, clearly disappointed with the answer. "I'd like to speak with your group after class about the cave incident," he told them and they took their seats.

The rest of the class went fairly quickly. The other six groups presented their findings and observations. One boy, Zach Scott, stood up with a random group because he was a new kid and hadn't actually gone on the trip. He looked so lost standing up at the front of the class awkwardly without a paper in his hand, and JJ couldn't help but feel like he knew this guy. He was five foot ten, brown skinned, with a freshly cut taper beside a head full of spiky black hair. He was lean, from sports most likely. Basketball or football and probably track or cross country. Despite everything, JJ noticed that they had the same exact eye color. Only JJ and his dad had the same colored eyes. The right eye, left half blue and right half golden brown. The left eye, right half green and left half gray. They could've been related except, that was impossible because JJ was an only child and he only had two cousins. *But those eyes.* Those eyes had an uncanny resemblance to his own. JJ made up his mind to talk to him at lunch.

The third lunch bell rang and all of the juniors rushed towards the lunchroom. The only eleventh graders not in the crowd swarming to stuff their faces with Friday's French Fries, the best food the school served, were Jericho, Cindy,

Charlotte, and JJ. As they remained seated they watched their teacher rise from his chair, walk across the room to the door, and close it. He turned the lock, trapping them in room 269A, and the interrogation began.

"Students," Arkaine said, putting on a smile clear as spring water, "Some *artifacts* were supposedly down in those caves. They are, um, *special,* to me."

Charlotte raised her hand then spoke. "Dr. Arkaine, we didn't find none of these supposed artifacts."
"Ms. Santiago," Arkaine snapped, slapping his hands down on a nearby desk. "Please refrain from lying. There are five of us in this room. Do any of you know what that means?" he asked, casting a questioning glare across the room.

Silence.

"It means that there are five people in this room who know that the story you all told is complete bullshit. Now, you all can tell me how the cave collapsed or else," he threatened.

"Or else," JJ laughed. "You can't do anything to us. Besides we told you what happened, the cave collapsed. End of story," he said.

"Well let's start a new chapter," Arkaine said before walking over to his scarred pine oak desk.

He opened the top drawer and grabbed out the Core that Jericho had left behind at the site yesterday. He placed it on the small wooden stool at the front of the room.

"Kids," Arkaine said, inhaling deeply, "There are five people here in this room. And now there's a Core," he said motioning to the pitch black stone. "Tell me, were there more Cores?" he demanded

"What's a Core?" Jericho asked, trying to be helpful and kill time.

"Boy, don't play dumb with me. I will not rest until I have them all, do you understand me?" Arkaine asked violently.

Just as Jericho was about to answer the question there was a knock on the door.

"Hello! Señor Arkaine! Are you in there?" Came the voice of Mr. Saez, a school custodian.

Dr. Arkaine hurriedly returned the Core to its hiding place then made an abrupt motion for the group of teens to stand before unlocking and opening the door. The custodian walked in with a broom and dust pan.

"Dismissed," Arkaine said, motioning for them to leave.

After the four of them escaped, they made their way to the cafeteria. At first they all said nothing and just walked in silence.

"Uh," Cindy said, getting the attention of everyone else, "Arkaine has a Core," she said.

Everybody stared waiting for her to continue. She didn't.

"And?" Charlotte asked.

"Oh," Cindy said loudly, regaining her train of thought. "This is bad. We have to tell your dad JJ. He might know what to do," she said, staring JJ down, while he avoided her eyes.

"Will you guys come to my house later when I tell him?" JJ asked everybody.

"Yeah," they all responded in unison.

"We'd never leave you hanging bro," Jericho said, punching JJ's arm playfully. "Now if you don't mind, I find that Friday's French Fries are calling my name," he said laughing, then dashed towards the cafeteria.

The rest of the group raced after him.

6

EVERYBODY CALLS ME JJ

◇ Zach Scott ◇

12:27 PM
The Cafeteria

The four of them inhaled heavily as they entered the cafeteria, the salty smell of Friday's French Fries filling their noses.

"Well if it isn't Justin and his entourage," Kathy, JJ's least favorite lunch lady, said as he approached the food bar.

"Hey Kathy, how are we doing today?" JJ asked sarcastically.

"It's Ms. Kathy."
"Ok well I guess I'll have pizza and fries."

"No more fries for twenty minutes and by then you'll be gone. You can still have sweet potatoes and spinach though Justin."

"It's JJ, Kathy. But I guess I'll have the sweet potatoes then," JJ said sullenly.

He was really looking forward to biting into hot, crispy, salty fries. He decided it was best to not think about them. They all got their food and headed to their usual table. Once they had all sat down and started eating, Jericho and Cindy got into a heated debate about which element was stronger, Air or Earth. Charlotte was scolding them, saying they needed to be quieter. JJ saw and heard none of it as he only had one thing on his mind. The new kid. *Where was he?* JJ's eyes scanned the mass of people devouring pizza and cheeseburgers. He was looking for a solid five minutes until a voice behind him broke his concentration.

"Excuse me," said a voice that was unfamiliar to JJ.

JJ turned around and there was a stranger staring back at him. Zach Scott. He was prodding JJ to move his bag out of the walkway so he could get to the empty corner table. JJ moved his bag.

"You going to that table?" JJ asked him, circling his hand in front of him motioning Zach to say his name.

"Zach."

"Right, Zach. But yeah, you going over to that table?" He asked again, pointing to the abandoned table.

"Mhmm."

"You can sit with us if you want to," JJ said, giving him a friendly smile.

Zach obliged and sat down to the left of JJ and the other three's conversation halted. They stared at Zach like he had three eyes. The three of them and Zach were in a heated staring match until Charlotte broke the tension.

"Hi. I'm Charlotte but you can call me Charlotte," she giggled.

Zach smiled. "I'm Zach."

"Well these two are Cindy and Jericho," she added motioning to the two.

Jericho waved. Cindy still sat quietly and stared.

When she finally realized everyone was staring at her she stuttered and said, "Oh, h-hey."

"Anyway. I'm Justin Joseph Rodriguez, but everybody calls me JJ," JJ introduced himself.

"Thanks for being so chill and letting me sit with you guys. Don't we have that archaeology elective together?" Zach asked.

"Yeah, but we call it Arkaine Arch," JJ told him and the group began laughing.

As they were laughing Zach threw in a fake chuckle although he had no idea what was funny.

Should I ask? Nah. I'm just gonna enjoy the fact that it's my first day, I have friends, and that mom found a job.

"Zach," Jericho said, slicing into Zach's thoughts.

"Yeah," Zach responded.

"Since it's a Friday and you're new to town plus we're your only friends-ow!" He exclaimed as Cindy stomped on his foot underneath the table.

"That was unnecessary," Jericho told her, addressing his hurt foot. "Anyway," he continued, "we're going to JJ's after school. You should ask your parents if you can come."

"My mom will probably want to meet your parents, JJ."

"Parent. Singular," JJ told him. "Just me and my dad. I'm sure he'd be willing and happy to meet her. He's a friendly dude."

"Awesome," Zach said.

Once they'd all finished their lunch they took up their trays then left the cafeteria, headed towards their fourth period.

3:45 PM
West San Diego High School

The end of the school day bell rang and all of the students and teachers rushed to their buses or cars. All except Dr. Arkaine. He was busy preparing for a little trip. His explosives would be going off soon and he needed to be there to see that his controlled chaos was actually controlled. He also knew that today would be his last at West

San Diego High. Now that he'd shown those kids that he had knowledge of the Core's existence and that he had a Core himself, he'd have to go into seclusion.

"Those bastard kids. They're messing up my plans. But now that they know I know, I can't stay," Arkaine finished monologuing and walked over to the old printer in the back of the classroom.

He pushed the two desks that were next to the printer a few feet away so he'd have space. He stared at the old machine and let out a long sigh. He wiped the dust from the numerical pad and input six numbers; 6-9-2-2-1-7. The top of the printer popped up a few inches and Arkaine lifted it up all of the way, revealing a secret safe. He removed the contents. A passport, a knapsack, and a laminated paper. He looked at the paper that had been sitting in the hidden lockspace for over five years.
It read:

Letter of Resignation

Arthur Malum Arkaine

To whom it may concern,

Due to unfortunate circumstances I am unable to continue adequately teaching at West San Diego High School and therefore am resigning my position. I apologize for the untimeliness and unexpected nature of this aforementioned resignation. It was an honor teaching at this institution for these past twelve years.

With best regards,

Dr. Arthur Arkaine

He went over to his desk and opened the middle right drawer and grabbed his car keys. He reached into the drawer above it and retrieved the black stone. Gently and cautiously he lifted the cover of his knapsack and placed the Core inside. He placed the resignation letter neatly on his desk and left the building.

"Arthur!" somebody yelled to him in the parking lot as he was getting into his car.

He turned around and saw Mayleen, the plump florid faced woman who worked the front desk in the main office.

"Have a nice weekend," she said waving.
Arkaine waved back and got in his black Jeep Cherokee. He turned the key in the ignition and the car roared to life. He shifted the car into drive, pulled out onto the road, and took off towards the cave site.

4:05 PM
Rodriguez Residence

JJ got out of his car and walked up the driveway to his house. He unlocked the front door and turned around, facing the driveway. His cherry red convertible Mustang and his father's daisy yellow Camaro sat side by side in it. He heard the front door open behind him.

"Hey Pop," JJ said.

"How was school?" his dad asked.

"Uh, it was okay I guess," he mumbled quickly.

"JJ. Why so dodgy?"

"How was your day?" He asked his dad, avoiding the question and hopefully buying a little time.

"Good. Two meetings. Nobody got fired today so that's a plus. We're working on developing a new ultra-reflective material for our new panel release that could possibly help cool houses in the future," he explained.

Just after he'd said that, cars pulled onto the curb in front of their house. Jericho's all white Honda still screeched like a banshee when he hit the brakes. Cindy came in right behind him in her tan Porsche that her parents bought for her a few months ago, so it was still looking practically brand new. Charlotte pulled up the rear in her blue Chevy, that was extra blinding in the California sun. JJ had to shield his eyes in order to see past the piercing glare.

"Hi kids," Mr. Rodriguez said from somewhere behind JJ, no longer still in the doorway.

"Hey Pops," Jericho yelled.

"Hey Uncle Anthony," Cindy and Charlotte said in unison. "Jinx!" They yelled. "Double jinx, triple jinx, quadruple jinx, quintuple jinx, infinity jinx. Pinch, poke you owe me a coke," they finished and burst into laughter.

Jericho walked up to JJ and gave him a fist bump and pointed to the girls.

"Can somebody say ex-tra," he said in a sing-song voice.

As they walked in the house, they hit the lock buttons on their keychains creating a short symphony of car alarms. They all grabbed a bottle of water from the refrigerator and took a seat at the kitchen counter as JJ's father made himself comfortable in the conjoining living room. Jericho, Cindy, and Charlotte all looked towards JJ, who made no effort to look up and acknowledge any of the stares from his friends.

"Fine!" He yelled. "Dad."

Mr. Rodriguez looked up from his book.

"Today something happened," JJ told him.

"Well what was it?" His dad asked him quickly, sounding concerned.

"I invited a friend over," he said with a guilty smile.

"JJ!" Charlotte yelled.

"Fine, fine," he said.

JJ gulped and took a deep breath.

"Pop. Arkaine kept us after class," he said, pausing.

"Go on," his dad encouraged.

"And he started asking us if we'd found artifacts. He was clearly talking about the Cores. All of us acted oblivious but I don't think he bought it. Scratch that. I know he didn't. Then he surprised us all by going over to his desk and getting the Core that Jericho dropped yesterday from one of the drawers. Then he put it at the front of the room like it wasn't nothing.
"Alright," was the only thing that Mr. Rodriguez said.

"Unc," Cindy said, "that's not all."

"What do you mean?" Mr. Rodriguez asked her.

"Well like he said Arkaine just put the Core on the stool like it was all good. Well I remembered something from the Core Planet story you told us, specifically about the Mayhem Core. It contained Chaos right?"

He nodded and said, "That's correct."

"Okay," she continued, "then he most definitely had that one."

"How can you be sure?"

"Well I'm like ninety-five percent sure if I remember the story right. If I could describe it to you, would you be able to know if it's the Chaos Core?"

"Mayhem Core and yes most definitely."

"Right, Mayhem. Sorry. Anyway, it was black and kind of bulgy. It had an ominous radiance about it. It had a distinct feature that was a dead giveaway."

"Which was?"

"I could see the places where it was fused together."

"That's definitely the Mayhem Core," he confirmed, hiding the fear creeping up the back of his neck.

"Well what does this mean, Pops?" Jericho asked, cutting into the conversation.

"I'm not sure," he confessed. "I'll need to go think on it in the study."

He started walking towards his office and as he was turning the doorknob about to walk in JJ remembered something.

"Wait, Pop," he called after his father.

"Yes?" His dad inquired.

"I wasn't kidding. I have a friend coming over with his parents to meet you. He, err, they just moved here. They should be here soon."

"What's your friend's name JJ?"

"Zach. Zach, uh," JJ stopped, trying to remember his new friend's last name.

"Scott," Cindy chimed.

"Yeah, that's it. Zach Scott."

Mr. Rodriguez stood so still it was as if he'd stared directly into the eyes of Medusa. The teens noticed him abruptly stop. They waited a few seconds for him to come out of this odd trance. JJ had enough waiting.

"Dad!" He yelled.

"JJ there's no need to yell, I'm right here," his father said.

"You ok?"

"Of course. I'm eager to meet the young man. Give me a shout when he and his mother arrive, will you?"

"Sure dad," JJ said to his father's back because Mr. Rodriguez was already walking into his study again.

The four of them got their drinks and sat down in the living room. Charlotte grabbed the TV remote and started flipping through the channels until she landed on a show explaining French fashion trends and sat the remote down. Jericho looked at JJ and made a face like, *really? This again?*

JJ took out his phone and waved it back and forth. He pressed the power button and the screen lit up with a picture of him and his two younger twin cousins, Janiah and Ronnie, at Disney three years ago. He'd always wanted a brother or sister. Being an only child he'd always had a spoiled childhood, but he'd always felt like something was missing. Ever since he could remember he'd been trying to figure out what it was and like always, he'd had no luck. He put in his six digit password: 0-6-2-8-0-7, the day he knew that he liked Charlotte Santiago. His lock screen faded away and revealed countless apps. He clicked on his favorite game, Temple Run 2. He mindlessly began swiping the screen up and down, left and right. He would tilt it occasionally to collect extra coins and power-ups. He was approaching his high score when a knock on the front door caused him to look up from his phone. When he looked back down at the screen, Barry Bones hit a log and was caught by the beast.

JJ got up and opened the door and Zach was standing there with a woman, who JJ presumed to be Zach's mother since he looked so much like her. She had a perfectly sculpted face, as if God had taken his time carving out each feature perfectly. Her only erratic feature was her eyes, the right was sapphire blue and the left was a brilliant shade of topaz. Her voice was as soft as a summer breeze.

She politely said, "Hello, my name is Pam. Are you JJ or did Zachary tell me the wrong house?"

She outstretched her hand to JJ which he took in his and shook gently before inviting them into his house.

"Dad!" JJ called to his father in his office. "They're here!"

JJ, Zach, and Pam all took a seat in the kitchen. As they waited for JJ's father to come out and greet them, JJ got them all some raspberry tea. No sooner had he poured the last cup, his father's office door opened and his dad walked out. He approached Zach and his mother while his son put the tea back in the refrigerator. He extended a hand to Ms. Scott and she shook it.

"Hello, I'm Anthony. I'm JJ's father and welcome to our home," Mr. Rodriguez said.

"Hello Anthony," Pam said smiling, showing rows of teeth whiter than cumulus clouds. "I'm Pam, Zach's mother. He says that your son, JJ, invited him to come over here for a little while today at school."

"That's correct."

He looked at JJ who was drinking his tea while staring at his phone.

"He's a nice, outgoing kid," he told her, "but he forgets to ask sometimes."

"Oh, is it a problem?"

"Not at all. It's nice to have a new addition to the teenagers that hang around," he joked.

"Okay then," she said and turned to look at her son. "Call me if you need me. You can stay as long as you want since it's a Friday. Have fun, okay," she finished her instructions and kissed him on the forehead.

She waved to everyone as she left out of the front door. As soon as she left, JJ asked Zach if he liked Tom Clancy games.

"No, not really. I mostly work out when I have free time, you know?" Zach asked.

"You lift?" JJ asked excitedly.

"Oh yeah."

"I've got weights in the basement if you're up to it.

"I'm game."

They started walking to the basement but JJ stopped in front of the door. He raised his pointer finger in front of Zach, halting him.

"What's up?" Zach asked.

"You guys coming?" JJ asked the other three and accidentally ignored the question he'd been asked.

Jericho clicked the power button on his phone and got up from the sofa where he'd been sitting. He walked over to the guys and JJ repeated his question.

"Are ya coming?"

"We'll be down in a few," Charlotte told him.

"Don't wait up," Cindy said.

6:40 PM
The Basement a.k.a. The Split

The three guys walked down the stairs to the room below. JJ walked over to his personal desk, even though it was pitch black. He knew the whole room like the back of his hand. He sat down in the chair.

"Jerry, do the lights," he asked Jericho.

Jericho clapped a rhythm into the darkness. Clap! Clap! Cla-clap! Clap! The lights flicked on and Zach saw JJ sitting at the desk.

"How'd you know exactly where that desk and chair were?" Zach asked JJ.

"I know the Split backwards and upside down," he replied.

"What's the Split?"

"You're standing in it. My basement is the gang's official hangout spot and we've dubbed it, the Split."

"Ah," Zach ogled sarcastically.

"So are we lifting or what?"

"Definitely."

7

THANKFUL!

◊ Please, Somebody Tell Me I'm Not Tripping ◊

6:45 PM
The Split

The Split was a cross between a high school weight room and an ultimate gaming hangout. You could only tell where one side split from the other by a length of shiny red duct tape that stretched out across the center of the floor. To the left of the tape there were dumbbells and barbells. JJ had two bench presses, a treadmill, and an elliptical. Yoga mats lined the walls along with stackable stepping stairs and a rack with towels that all had 'Justin Joseph' embroidered into them. To the right of the stripe there were shelves and shelves of Xbox 360, Xbox One, PlayStation 3, PlayStation 4, and Wii U games lining the walls, accompanied by the corresponding systems and headsets. The middle of the right wall was hidden by a 55" Toshiba flat screen TV. In the far right corner four white laptops were closed and arranged symmetrically into a rectangle atop a circular wooden table.

The walls had posters of various video games and game characters. It was truly a sanctuary for hardcore gamers and the workout obsessed.

After about an hour of JJ and Zach's intense working out, Jericho looked up from behind one of the laptops at the circle table and asked JJ to come over. Zach stopped working out, grabbed a towel, and watched the guys from across the room. Jericho whispered something in JJ's ear which made him stop and think hard for a moment, then he looked back at Jericho and shrugged his shoulders. JJ opened his mouth to say something but was stopped when the Split's door was thrown open by Cindy who was fleeing down the stairs with Charlotte on her heels. They rushed over to the TV and pressed the power button and light spilled over the whole room. The girls started arguing over the remote.

"Gimme it," Cindy demanded.

"No. It doesn't matter who has it because we're both going to turn to the same channel," Charlotte argued.

"Yes it does."

"Why? Exactly, it doesn't," she concluded, snatching the remote away.

"Fine, just change the channel."

Charlotte pressed the number -3- button on the remote and a live news action report was on with a caption that read, "Cave explosion leaves one dead, body yet to be found."

The reporter was in mid-sentence, "-where a devastating event took place recently. Behind me you'll see what remains of Winifred Caverns once called the Diamond Points because of Alfred Winifred, who discovered the stalactites and stalagmites contained diamonds. Well here in those very caves," the reporter motioned behind himself at the destruction, "a massive explosion has turned them completely to rubble. It is said to have been caused by a large, concentrated timed explosive device that detonated less than an hour ago. Nearby residents who reported the incident say that they'd only seen two buses and a black jeep visit the caves within the last forty eight hours. It was said that the buses arrived yesterday and the jeep today, shortly before the explosions went off. Pieces of the jeep and a license plate were recovered and it is said to have been registered to an Arthur Arkaine Ph.D. Dr. Arkaine's body has yet to be recovered but as of now the investigators are presuming him dead on the scene. If you have any information on the events that have occurred here or of Arthur Arkaine's present whereabouts, please call 1-800-281-7863. This is Orville Burrell, News Channel 3. Back to you Don."

The tv switched from Orville Burrell's face to Don Denton, an early night time newscaster, who recapped everything Burrell had just said and then started talking about the next story. Charlotte pressed the power button on the remote and the tv blinked to a black screen. Everybody sat in silence until Zach broke through the quiet.

"Damn," he swore. "Y'all were just there yesterday right?" he asked.

Jericho nodded his head.

"Do you realize how thankful you should be?" he asked, looking around the room.

"Thankful!" Charlotte exploded. "A man just died in an explosion but, nah, let's all just be thankful!"

"Letty," Cindy said carefully.

"What?" Charlotte yelled.

"Chill."

"Zach. What do you mean we should be thankful?" Jericho asked him.

"Well, the news guy said that the explosion was caused by a time bomb. Nobody knows who set 'em or how long they'd been there. You guys could've been done-zo. When I said be thankful, it wasn't in regards to some stupid archaeology teacher that died, it was because you guys were there and those deaths could've been yours. I meant no disrespect to Dr. Arkaine, hell I didn't even know the guy," Zach explained.

"Okay I got you. I'm sorry for snapping on you like that," Charlotte apologized.

"It's cool. It's really not even that deep," he said reassuringly.

Jericho cleared his throat which directed everyone's attention to him. He was about to say something but only an "uh" sound came out. He stared at JJ so intensely that a hole may've been formed in JJ's head if he didn't stop him.

"What?!" JJ asked, shouting the question.

Jericho quickly said, "the thing," and then looked at Zach before darting his eyes back to JJ.

"Oh yeah," JJ said, facepalming. "You two, come here," he told Cindy and Charlotte.

JJ turned his back to Zach, who was now sitting in an old burgundy recliner on the gaming side of The Split. Zach stared at JJ's back as he whispered to the two girls.

While he whispered, he clearly said something that exasperated Charlotte because she threw her hands up and spun in a three-sixty.

"No!" Charlotte yelled, "I don't think it's a good idea!"
"Jerry, a little help," JJ pleaded.

Jericho walked over to the group huddled together. Zach sat quietly listening and watching the whole time. He picked up on a few words; bad, shouldn't, cool, powers, and something that sounded like decors. Zach grew tired of the secrecy and snapped.

"Why the hell are you guys being so secretive?!" He shouted. "Like, I know y'all are talking about me in some way or another otherwise you would just be talking out loud! Timidity does not equal stupidity!"

In a soothing voice, Cindy said, "Zach, we know you're not stupid. We'd never just automatically think that of somebody. I'll apologize for everybody because we didn't mean to offend you. Our bad."

"I'm sorry too," Zach apologized. "Y'all have been really cool and I just snapped, but for real, what are y'all talking about?"

They gave each other awkward looks and by accident, they all got into a heated staring match. Zach thought that they might stand there forever if he didn't intervene.
"Ahem. Not all at once please. And if somebody could tell me today that'd be great," Zach snidely remarked.

"Okay," Jericho said. "JJ has something he wants to tell you."

Jericho shoved JJ and he stumbled forward. Jericho looked at JJ with a blank expression as if he didn't know that he'd just put all the pressure on him.

"Zach," JJ started.

"What's up?" Zach inquired back.

"I'm going to keep it real with you. Are you cool with that?"

"That would probably be helpful, yeah."

"Okay, fine. There's only one way you'll even remotely believe that I'm not insane. I've got a question for you."
"Shoot."

"You like superheroes?"

"Do apples grow on trees? Hell yeah I do. Marvel over DC but hell yeah."

"Good. That's good to know."

"Literally had nothing to do with anything bruh."

"Just come here," he groaned at Zach, who arose from his chair.

JJ walked over to the desk and sat down in the red rolling office chair. Zach walked across the room and grabbed a few stepping stairs. He stacked them up on the floor beside JJ and watched him remove a beige cloth from atop a small locked mahogany box.

"Before you open that box right there," Zach said as JJ lifted a small silver key to the lock, "tell me what's in there."

"Something or rather *some things* of value to some people," JJ said, inserting the key into the box and unlocking it. Slowly he opened the lid.

"Rocks?" Zach asked, confused by the box's contents.

JJ rolled his eyes and said, "Yeah but they're *special* rocks. Only certain people think so though, everyone else thinks they're regular pretty rocks."

"So what do you all think?"

"They're pretty special," he told him and everyone else concurred.

"Alright then," Zach said. "How will I decide if they're special or not?"

"Simple. Just pick them up one by one. If you don't think they're special then just put them back. Think you can handle it?"

"I'm game," Zach said, picking up the green pyramid shaped stone and moving it around between his fingers.

He flipped it into the air like a quarter and caught it. He twirled it this way and that, trying to find out if it was special or not. After two minutes he was pretty sure that it was not and became bored. "Still don't know if it's a regular rock or a special rock," he yawned.

"Just grab the next one," JJ told him.

"Alright," he said, grabbing the transparent polygonal stone.

He repeated the same procedure as before, moving the stone around in his hands. He tossed it back and forth, from left hand to right hand and back to left again. He sneezed really hard and accidentally dropped the stone. Just before it hit the floor Jericho swiped his hand up and a small gust of air blew the stone back up onto the desk. Everybody except Zach, who was recovering from his sneeze, looked at Jericho, whose eyes were fading from glowing white back to normal, while he smiled nervously and said, "next one."

"Yeah, that's a good idea," JJ said, secretly praying Zach hadn't seen any of that.

"Whoa, this may sound strange," Zach said as he picked up the final rock, "but this one feels really warm. Like it was, heated up or something."

He was holding a stone that was almost spherical except for a straight edge that allowed it to sit flat on its side. It was blacker than night and the darkness was only interrupted by a dark swirl of orange. If Zach didn't know better he would've sworn that the orange spiral was revolving around the stone's glossy blackness.

Although, JJ did say they were special to some people and not others so there may be a chance, he thought. Anyway, let me mess around with this rock so these weirdos will stop staring at me like I'm from a different planet or something.

Zach put the stone in his right hand and pretended to throw the rock as if it were a football. He tossed it lightly into the air and caught the pass he'd thrown to himself, then he celebrated the touchdown.

"Okay, so if you'd kindly reiterate why you wasted like ten minutes of my life when I could've been lifting. Nope. Y'all just got me looking stupid holding some funny colored rocks. Y'all some straight up weirdos, real talk," Zach ranted and stood up. "And to top it all off-," he started, but his sentence got choked in the back of his throat.
His eyes started glowing orange and his pupils gravitated upwards, moving towards the back of his head. His body was as stiff as a board and he stood motionless in front of the four others. Then, out of nowhere, Zach's body started steaming and this made everybody else in the room back away cautiously.

"This definitely didn't happen to any of us!" Cindy yelled as she backed away.

"Give it up for Captain Obvious," Charlotte said sarcastically.

"Really?" Jericho asked. "You really think now is a good time to be facetious?"

"Sorry," she apologized, "but look."

A thick gray cloud of odorless smoke had formed above Zach's head and began descending slowly over his body. When the cloud settled at his feet, his eyes stopped glowing and turned completely white and then back to their original colors. The cloud dissipated and left Zach standing in front of the others looking confused. They were staring back at him, speechless.

"What?" Zach asked. "Wait. Why do I feel so-," he paused to think of the word he wanted to use, "-peculiar?"

JJ said, "Well, I'm gonna give it to you straight. You're a Core Elementalist."

Zach stared at him, waiting for him to elaborate.

"You know those superheroes we were talking about?" JJ asked him.

Zach nodded his head.

"Well now you're one of them. Just like us," he finished and motioned toward the three of his friends and himself.

"A superhero," Zach repeated. "No way. I don't believe it. No amount of smooth talking, fancy rocks, and magic tricks are gonna make me think otherwise. There's no way you guys have superpowers."

As soon as the words left his lips, the lights went out. Not just the light fixtures, but it seemed as if all the light had been sucked out of the room. Not even their phones would turn on.
"Not just them," came a voice slicing through the darkness, followed by the slits of yellow eyes. "Me as well."

"Mr. Rodriguez, is that you?" Zach asked the voice.

"Yes," Mr. Rodriguez answered.

"Do you know why it's so dark in here?"

"That depends," Mr. Rodriguez replied and fully opened his eyes, revealing their intense yellow glow. His deep yellow aura swayed around him, lighting up the staircase as he continued his descent.

"Does everyone see that?" Zach asked his friends.

Nobody responded.

"Please, somebody tell me I'm not tripping," Zach pleaded.

Still, he got no response.

"Abra-cadabra," Mr. Rodriguez whispered loudly and opened his hand wide.

A bright scalding white light emerged from the palm of his hand. Everybody had to avert their eyes but not before yelling, "ah!" The brightness dimmed after several moments and once he had everyone's attention, JJ's father dipped his hand through the air and shoved it upward. The ball of light glided from his hand and split up, entering all of the bulbs, phones, gaming systems, and the tv. Everybody watched as the light jumped into everything, filling out the darkness. They looked up at Mr. Rodriguez, staring in either amazement or confusion.

"How'd you-" Zach started to ask shakily but was interrupted by Mr. Rodriguez.

"-How's that for a magic trick?" He asked, smirking proudly.

Mr. Rodriguez walked away from the staircase, excused his son from his seat, and sat down in JJ's office chair. He looked up to the ceiling and closed his eyes.

"Uh, dad," JJ said frantically. "We've got a little bit of a situation here."

"Which is?" His dad inquired, his eyes still closed.

"Zach. He, uh. Well. He maybe sort of. You know. There's a possibility he could've-," JJ rambled.

"-Dude, spit it out already," Jericho interrupted.

"He bonded with a Core," JJ said. "There! You happy?" He asked Jericho.

Jericho started to give JJ the finger when he realized that JJ's dad was now up on his feet looking directly at him, so instead he smoothed his hand through his hair and allowed the conversation to continue.

"Obviously, why else would I have come into the Split in such a dramatic fashion? Was it the Magma, Vega, or Arctic Core?" Mr. Rodriguez asked anybody who knew what he was talking about.

"Wait. They have names now?" Cindy asked.

"Oh. Yes they have names now," Mr. Rodriguez replied.

"So which is which?" Charlotte asked, cutting in.

"Green is Vega, clear is Arctic, and the black and orange is Magma," he told her.

"Magma," Charlotte assured him.

Mr. Rodriguez's eyes widened for a split second but he quickly regained his composure.

"Has anybody explained what has just happened to Mr. Scott?" He asked.

"They said I was a superhero," Zach offered.

Everyone pointed to JJ, placing all the blame on him. Mr. Rodriguez scowled at JJ and squinted his eyes at him until JJ finally said something.

"First of all, I think I said he was *like* a superhero," JJ clarified. "Second, I would just like to state that my friends, suck."
"Well let's just say you now have abilities to save from dramatics," Mr. Rodriguez said. "You've bonded with a Core, the Magma Core to be exact. This means the Lava Elemental has chosen you to be its Elementalist and you'll be able to conjure and manipulate lava, first and foremost. In time you should be able to widen your elemental manipulation as your abilities develop.

There's potential for volcanic manipulation, Light told Mr. Rodriguez.

I was just thinking that, Mr. Rodriguez said back, *but I think I should let him discover that on his own. He isn't even fully aware of the hand he's just been dealt.*

True. Very True.

"You'll also have to learn how to use your abilities properly. The Core Elementals are of ancient extraterrestrial descent and with them comes powerful potential. They were once giant beings of pure energy but now, in their current state, they must choose a host to bond with. The Lava Elemental chose you for a reason, just as our Elementals have chosen us. I myself have the Lambent Core and was chosen by the Light Elemental."

"I have the Pyro Core. Got chose by the Fire Elemental," JJ told Zach through a proud beaming smile.

"I've got the Aquarius Core, Water Elemental," Charlotte said.

Zach just sat there, staring enigmatically, being shocked by all of the impossible information.

"Turbulent Core, Air Elemental," Jericho said after Charlotte.

"And last but not least there's me. I was lucky and bonded with the Terra Core, which means I got the Earth Elemental," Cindy said with a smile.

After a few minutes of nobody saying anything Zach finally found his words.

"Okay so let me see if I've got this straight," he said, clearing his throat. He pointed at JJ and continued, "you can control fire?" Then he pointed at Charlotte, "you can control water?" He switched his finger pointing over to Cindy and said, "you earth," then he pointed at Jericho, "you air," and finally looked over at Mr. Rodriguez and said, "and you light? All because giant space aliens made of energy took residency?"

They all nodded.

JJ looked at Zach and pointed at him. "And you lava," he told him.

"Zach," Mr. Rodriguez said, getting Zach's attention. Once he saw he had it, he continued, "Tomorrow I am taking everyone on a trip to further their understanding of their abilities. Feel free to tag along with us, if you'd like."

"I dunno man, this all still sounds a little too wild," Zach confessed. "Like, I've been running all of this stuff through my head and I just can't begin to wrap my mind around it all."

"I do have quite a bit of information on the subject I could offer you, if you'd like," Mr. Rodriguez suggested.

"I guess so," Zach agreed, not really sounding too sure about the offer.

"Let me tell you about some elements on a distant planet," Mr. Rodriguez told him, "It may help to put things into perspective. I think it's time you learned the Legend of the Core."

"A fable?" He asked skeptically.

"A recollection of events," JJ's dad corrected, his face dead serious.

He closed his eyes and all of the lights in the room faded away once more. When he opened them a bright aurora of light burst into existence in front of him. As his aura swayed and he readied himself to begin, Cindy started to screech quietly to herself. Charlotte smiled at her friend's giddiness.

"What?" She whispered to her.

"I can't help it," Cindy whispered back. "Everytime he uses his powers I just get so damn excited. It's like we're living in a freaking movie, man."

Zach stared intently as JJ's dad spoke and the aurora illustrated his words.

"A long time ago, eons before our world even existed, there was only one thing in existence. The Core Being..."

8

POOL OF SHADOWS

◇ What's Happening To Me? ◇

5:45 PM

Winifred Caverns

Arthur checked his watch as he barreled down the road, which read 5:45.

"Fifteen minutes," Arthur said aloud to himself.

He screeched into the parking section at the cave sites, which was barren except for leaves blowing in the wind. He grabbed the knapsack from where it lay in the front passenger seat and carefully felt around inside for the stone. Once he was made sure that it was still safe, he pulled the handle on his door and got out of the car. He calmly walked towards the cave sites, looking over his shoulder repeatedly to make sure nobody was following him. Although he knew nobody was after him, he couldn't help feeling as though he were being followed or at the very least watched. He approached the first cave and checked his watch again. *Five fifty-two.*

"Eight minutes to set up and make sure everything runs smoothly. I hope everything goes as planned because I really can't afford to fuck this up," He said to himself.

He walked away from the caves and positioned himself on a hill that overlooked the sites before checking his watch for a third time. *Five fifty-nine.* He covered his ears and shut his eyes tight, awaiting the first of the explosions to happen. He sat on the hill with his ears covered and his face cringed for several minutes. He unscrunched his face and took his hands from his ears. He listened but heard nothing. Again he checked his watch. *Six eleven.* He became infuriated.
"No!" He yelled. "Why am I not seeing rubble? Why are there no loud booms of exploding time bombs? Why is there no destruction?" He asked himself loudly.

His entire body was shaking with anger.

"I'm gonna be pissed if I walk down into those caves and they blow up. I'm really not trying to die today. That'd really, fucking, suck," he droned.

He walked down into the closest cave and luckily it didn't blow up when he went in. He found the time charge and the countdown timer was on zero. *Strange that the time ran out but the bomb didn't explode,* Arthur thought. He plucked the bomb from the wall as he left the cave and entered the cave to his right. Again he wasn't blown up, but when he found the bomb, he found the time had run out again, just as the last. He left and checked the other caves and found that all of the bombs had done the same thing. When he had finished searching the last cave, he placed the pile of duds at his feet. They didn't do anything except add to the anger that was now bubbling up inside of Arthur. He sat down on an outcropping rock and tried to calm down. He took the black stone out of the knapsack and started taking deep breaths. So many thoughts rushed through his mind.

Those stupid teenagers who had found the Core. The fact that he had to quit his job. All the years he'd spent looking for the Cores. Wait, are there more Cores? Do the kids have them? Do they even know what they are?

All the while he was thinking about these things he was moving the black Core around in his hands. With every new thought he became more enraged. His calm deep breaths had changed into quick short ones without him even noticing. His teeth were clenched tight as one last thought crossed his mind. *This is all Anthony's fault.* With that thought he opened his mouth and let out a long shout that echoed off of the cave walls and resonated for minutes. The Core suddenly started releasing a thick black gloom. Arthur stared down at it in disbelief.

"Finally," he said, relieved.

The darkness slithered up his arms and started covering his body like a swarm of ants. Arthur's body arose from the rock where he was sitting and he closed his eyes. He stayed suspended in the air for moments, then he dropped and landed upright on both feet with his eyes still closed. The blackness faded from Arthur's body. As he stood there, something even stranger began to happen. Shadows from all around started meandering into the cave and lingering around Arthur. In addition to his own shadow, shadows from everywhere and everything streamed like water into the cave and gathered at his feet. Minutes passed and Arthur was now standing atop a pool of shadows that weren't entirely his own. They snaked their way up his legs and thighs. They covered his waist and torso, then spread upwards over his chest. Finally, the shadows slid up his neck before enveloping his entire face. He stood there, a shadowy figure, simply looming over the cave's emptiness. All around him the ground began to tremble and the walls began crumbling inward. Slabs of rock fell from the crumbling walls and ceiling, crashing into the quaking ground. The ground beneath Arthur's feet began cracking, the cracks growing and spreading throughout the floor. The shadows melted from off of Arthur's skin and reformed beneath his feet.

Arthur opened his mouth and let loose a loud guttural rumble from the depths of his soul. The cave walls shot outward, exploding all around Arthur. The force of the explosion was so intense that the surrounding caves were blown to rubble. Arthur was radiating energy. He ceased the rumbling. He opened his eyes, which now were glazed over, blacker than tar, and observed the surrounding area. The shockwave he'd caused left him standing in a thirty foot wide crater. Although a crater had formed and extensive damage had been caused, he stood unfazed and unharmed on top of his shadow pool. Arthur noticed one of the cave entrances still looked very much intact. *I can fix that.* He opened his mouth to let out another guttural roar in the direction of the still standing caves. The force was enough to make the caves shudder fiercely and crumble slightly, but Arthur stopped abruptly. He fell to his knees and suddenly felt cold and clammy. He felt, powerless.

"What's happening to me?" He shouted, his fear almost palpable. "This didn't happen to Anthony!"
Arthur tried to stand up but lost his balance and fell backwards, smacking his head against the jagged

ground below. The shadows he was laying on descended and began forming a shell over him again. They covered the entire surface of his body and Arthur slipped into unconsciousness. After he passed out the shadows began compressing his body. They compressed and shrank until they vanished into nothingness, Arthur disappearing with them.

9

WHAT THE HECK IS A CETOBA?

◇ Training Day ◇ Part 1 ◇ CETOBA ◇

9:36 AM

JJ's Room

JJ opened his eyes to darkness. He pulled his red and black striped blanket from over his face. Blinking his eyes to adjust to the light of morning, he surveyed his room. He saw Jericho sitting up against his bed eating cereal and watching TV. No matter how late Jericho stayed up, he always woke up at six forty-five on the dot. His brain was like an alarm clock that had been programmed. The next thing JJ noticed was the white duffel bag that was sitting on the floor next to his best friend.

"Ay," JJ mumbled to Jericho.

Jericho looked away from the TV and turned his head towards JJ.

"You're up," Jericho said.

JJ threw his arm over the side of the bed and pointed at the bag with his pinky finger.

"You know it's," he paused to check his watch, "Nine thirty-six. You should work on getting up earlier."

"What's in the bag you fucking robot?" JJ asked, yawning the question and insult.

"Stuff," he replied. "Your dad packed them. Unless somebody perfectly copied your dad's handwriting. There's a whole bunch of bags downstairs, this one had my name on it."

"I got one?"

"Probably. Get up though. Your lazy ass has already slept past nine."

"Make me. Not everyone can wake up at six thirty, get a bowl of cereal, and watch freaking cartoons till noon."

"First, I get up at six forty-five. Second, I take a pee before I get my cereal. Third, it's only like, nine thirty-sevenish. Fourth and final, before you try to be sarcastic you should get your lazy butt up."

"Ugh."

JJ sat up on his bed, scratched his head, and yawned again. He got up off his bed and walked past Jericho out of his bedroom. He went to the bathroom before heading downstairs to the kitchen. When he got there he found his father, Charlotte, and Cindy sitting at the counter eating cereal and discussing his dad's powers.

"How long did it take to do that light-holding thing from last night?" Cindy asked enthusiastically.

"Actually that was one of the first tricks I learned how to do. Although, it's been quite some time since I've had the chance to perform it. Did you enjoy it?" He asked both of the girls.

"Yeah. It was pretty freaking awesome," Charlotte told him.

"Morning everybody," JJ said to them.

"Good morning," his father said.

"Hey JJ," Cindy said.

"Morning to you too," Charlotte replied.

JJ grabbed a porcelain bowl from the cabinet, a box of cereal from atop the fridge, and some milk. After he fixed himself a bowl of cereal he took a seat at the counter beside Charlotte. JJ crunched on his cereal as the other three who were sitting at the counter continued their conversation. He managed to tune them out and stared at the bags sitting on the floor by the door. When he finally finished his breakfast, he asked the question that had been nagging at him the whole time he'd been eating.

"What's in the bags?" He asked his dad, who was still in the midst of his own conversation.

"Say again?" His father asked.

"The bags. What's in them?"

"Just some things you might need for today's trip."

"Vague, but okay. Which one's mine?"

"The one closest to the wall."

JJ walked over to where the four bags were sitting. He looked down and read the tag.

Justin Joseph - Fire Elementalist - Pyro Core

The other three belonged to Cindy, Charlotte, and, to JJ's surprise, Zach. He grabbed his bag and climbed the stairs.

"Justin," his dad called up to him, "you didn't put away your dishes."

"My fault," JJ apologized.

JJ dropped the bag at the base of the stairs and walked back over to the counter. He grabbed his bowl and spoon, rinsed them off in the sink, then put them in the dishwasher. He went and grabbed his bag again before heading upstairs. When he got back into his room he dropped the bag at the door and sat down on his bed. Jericho was flipping through channels trying to find the best cartoons.

"If I didn't know you better, I'd say you were a five year old trapped in a sixteen year old's body," JJ told Jericho.

"If I didn't know you better, I'd say you are going to be ready to leave with everybody else in," Jericho paused to check the time, "four minutes."

"You know that I'm never on time for anything except lunch."

The two friends laughed. JJ got up and walked over to the closet. He grabbed the first shirt he touched, a short sleeve gray shirt, and threw it on. He walked over to his dresser and grabbed a pair of acid washed jeans and threw them on. He put his red and white Adidas on before picking up the bag and walking to the door.

"Come on and don't forget the bowl. My dad's always giving me shit about leaving dishes in my room," JJ told Jericho.

"Okay, I'm right behind you," Jericho told him. "Not like you're in any rush though," he mumbled. "It's ten twelve by the way."

"Don't care. Let's go."

The two of them walked downstairs to find JJ's dad, Charlotte, and Cindy waiting for them by the front door. The girls were gripping bags identical to the ones the boys carried. As they waited for Jericho to put his dishes in the dishwasher JJ asked his father a question.

"Are we driving our cars and following you or," his question momentarily trailed off, "how's this gonna work exactly?"

"Actually, no. We're all riding together and I'm driving," his dad replied.

"We're not all going to fit in your Camaro Pop."

"Duh Justin. Of course I realized that five of us won't fit in my sports car so I went out and bought an Escalade."

"An Escalade? Seriously?"

"Seriously," he said, nodding his head.

The group walked outside and saw a brand new gray Escalade sitting at the edge of the driveway. They put their bags into the trunk and piled into the vehicle. After Mr. Rodriguez started the car he spoke to everyone.

"Okay guys and girls, first things first. Everyone needs to buckle up if you haven't already," he said. After everyone's buckle clicked he continued, "second this is gonna be a lengthy trip, so please make sure you've got everything."

Everyone searched themselves to make sure they had everything that they needed. Once everybody confirmed that they had everything he put the car in drive.

"Let's get this show on the road."

12:30 PM
Somewhere in Palm Desert

"Miss Thompson," Mr. Rodriguez called over his shoulder, "remember when I told you that when we arrived I'd tell you?" he asked.

"Indeed I do," Cindy replied.

"We have officially arrived."

Mr. Rodriguez parked the vehicle on a sandy desert plain in the middle of nowhere. He woke up his son who had been sleeping in the front passenger seat. It took several shakes to wake JJ up. Once he lifted his head, he started rubbing the kinks out of his neck and cast a confused look out of the windshield.

"Where the heck are we?" He asked, turning around to see more desert matching the one he saw in front of him.

"Well once everybody exits the car, I'll explain. Technically speaking, I guess you could say we're in Palm Desert," his dad told him.

They each got their bags from the trunk once they stepped out of the car and into the arid desert. Everyone kept surveying the area to try to decipher why they were standing in the middle of dry, sweltering nowhere.

"Okay everyone, let's go," JJ's dad told everyone before he started walking off into the desert. "Oops, almost forgot."

He raised his hands in the direction of the Escalade as his eyes and aura lit up. The other four watched in amazement as the car dematerialized right in front of their eyes. They couldn't help but stare at JJ's dad in awe.
"Just another magic trick," he said modestly as his eyes returned to normal.

The four of them slowly started after Mr. Rodriguez, who had already turned around and continued walking. They blindly followed him through the desert, constantly looking back at the spot where the invisible Escalade stood. After a few minutes Jericho started getting antsy and asked the question that was on everyone's mind.

"Unc, where are we going?"

Mr. Rodriguez casually pointed into the distance and said, "there."

Charlotte spoke up, "excuse me but, there's nothing there."

"Nothing there?" Mr. Rodriguez questioned Charlotte's statement. "How can you not see the-." He stopped mid-sentence. "You all can't see the base, can you?"

They informed him that they could not.

"Okay. I have another trick to show you," Mr. Rodriguez told them.

"Well what is it?" JJ asked.

"Show us," Cindy pleaded.

"Close your eyes," Mr. Rodriguez instructed.

After everyone closed their eyes he spoke again.
"You'll feel a slight tingle while I give you The Vision. Open your eyes slowly when I give you the go ahead," he told them.

"What's The Vision?" Jericho asked.

"It's, how you kids say nowadays, lit fam," Mr. Rodriguez responded. "Just wait and you'll see."

JJ opened his left eye and peeked at his dad.

"Justin. Close your eyes," Mr. Rodriguez said sternly.

Once his son was properly following the directions, he put both of his hands out in the air towards the teenagers. He squinted his eyes and focused on them. His eyesight started to change from his normal 20/20 vision into black and white. Then all of the color faded entirely and his eyesight went completely black. When his vision returned he was staring at red, orange, yellow, blue, and white clones of the teenagers. All he could see was their heat signatures. A buzzing white light ignited at the tips of his fingers and he waved his hands in front of the four heads in front of him. The light jumped from his fingers onto the other's eyelids.

"Ooh! It is tingly," Charlotte said. "I kinda like it."

After a few moments had passed and the light had dissipated, Mr. Rodriguez spoke to them.

"Now slowly open your eyes. Slowly," he said calmly.

They all cautiously began to lift their eyelids, but nothing had changed. They still saw the same exact desert they'd seen before closing their eyes. JJ was extremely confused.

"That didn't do anything," he told his dad.

"Look again," his dad told him.

They all stared hard out into the desert's vast emptiness and again they still saw absolutely nothing. Mr. Rodriguez could see the frustration blooming on their faces so he decided that he'd give them some more insight about The Vision.

"You can all stop. There's another thing I have to mention to you all. Your vision has been slightly altered," he said to them. "I have the ability to see the world as if, through different lenses. I can see infrared as well as black and white. I can separate colors to single out one specifically or exclude one from my sight. Also, in the darkness I am able to see perfectly. It's almost like looking through night vision goggles, except everything looks normal. I also possess the ability to pass on these alterations to others, which is what I've just done to all of you."

JJ, Jericho, Cindy, and Charlotte stared at JJ's dad with blank faces. It was hard to believe that the man could literally change how he viewed the world. Even harder to believe was that he'd made it so that they could do it too. They all had questions but not one of them could find their tongues.

"It's a cycle," Mr. Rodriguez told them. "Black and white will come first. Then infrared. Then night vision. Now, why don't you all try again. This time, really try to focus on seeing black and white. When you do see it, try to go a step further and see infrared. You'll only need to make it that far in order to see CETOBA."

"What the heck is a CETOBA?" Cindy asked, genuinely baffled.

"Well, CETOBA is a secret facility that was built by the original Core Elementalists as a safe haven. CETOBA is an acronym for, Core Elementalists Training and Operating Base of Action. As you can see it's much easier to say CETOBA than the entire mouthful version," Mr. Rodriguez explained. "Now, let's get to it."

10

THAT WAS WAY MORE THAN SLIGHTLY

◇ Mr. Umpter, You're On Deck ◇

1:00 PM
Outside CETOBA

"I'm stuck at the black and white," Jericho whined to everyone. "Everything looks like old-timey tv and as cool as that may seem, it's starting to get old. How do I get past this?"

"The opposite of the way you got stuck," JJ said laughing.

"You think this is funny?" Jericho asked, a little bit of anger biting at the end of the question.

"A little," JJ replied.

"C'mon Jericho," Charlotte said encouragingly, "it's simple. Focus on the heat waves you see. Then try to imagine everything transforming into heat waves. That's the way I did it."

"Okay. I'll try anything to get out of this heat," he told her.

"Speaking of heat, hurry up," Cindy said. "I'm going to have a heatstroke if we stand outside CETOBA any longer."

"I'm trying," Jericho said through gritted teeth.

"Don't rush him, geez," Charlotte told Cindy. "Just because it was easy for you doesn't mean you should be criticizing him because it's not as easy for him."

"Whatever," Cindy said, her face enigmatic.

Jericho searched for heat waves bouncing off of the grainy ground beneath his feet. He finally spotted the clear lines rippling away from the ground and concentrated on imagining everything as heat waves. JJ, Charlotte, Cindy, Mr. Rodriguez, the sand, even himself. His eyesight went completely black. He was sure his eyes were open, but he saw nothing.

"What the?" He yelled and shut his eyes.

He pressed fingers into his eye sockets before flinging his eyes back open. His gaze was met by an enormous building in front of him, radiating the most vibrant shade of red he'd ever seen. It was an extraordinary structure that was so expertly hidden that Jericho had no choice but to be impressed. Mr. Rodriguez was powerful and continually showed expertise in his abilities.

He is truly remarkable, Jericho thought.

"Does everyone see CETOBA?" Mr. Rodriguez asked.

After everyone confirmed that they could see CETOBA, Mr. Rodriguez let out a big sigh of relief.

"Okay, let's go in. Are you all ready?"

The four of them looked at one another, trying to find a mutual confirmation using facial expressions. After a minute, they came to a decision.

"No," JJ said.

Charlotte smacked him in the back of his head and called him a doofus.

"Ow! Okay. Fine, yes. Please take us in dad," JJ said to his father while he rubbed the back of his head.

"AVA, scan the Elementalists," Mr. Rodriguez requested loudly.

A large voice boomed all around them. The voice had a somewhat feminine tone but was also still very authoritative and stern.

The voice said, "Welcome to the Core Elementalists Training and Operating Base of Action, or CETOBA. I am the Attractive Voice Automaton or AVA. Vocal recognition activated. Vocal pattern recognized. Anthony James Rodriguez. Welcome back, Sir. How many Elementalists are present?" AVA asked.

"Five, including myself," he replied. "The other's Symbols are arriving shortly so for now you can just run the program to gather the rest of the information you need."

"Understood. Five complete identity diagnostics. Authorization code?"

"Chitty, chitty, bang, bang."

"Authorization code recognized. Scanning commenced. Please hold still."

Several seconds of utter silence from the group followed AVA's request. The only noise being made was the humming from CETOBA as it scanned the people in front of it.

"Personal Identity Scan and Core Identity Scan complete. Personal Identity Scan successful. Core Identity Scan, inconclusive. Anthony James Rodriguez, Lambent Core

Elementalist, Keeper of Light. Justin Joseph Rodriguez, Core identity unknown. Jericho Antwan Umpter, Core identity unknown. Cinthya Persephone Thompson, Core identity unknown. Charlotte Isabella Luna Santiago, Core identity unknown. All Elementalists internal biometrics monitoring. Access granted. Please enter CETOBA, Elementalists," AVA finished.

They all watched as the red doors of CETOBA slid aside to reveal a small blue foyer peeking out. The doors stopped moving and without hesitation they crossed the threshold.

1:40 PM

Inside CETOBA

"Now that we're inside you can turn your infrared off. You do it the same way you did it before. This room is darkened so that you won't be blinded when cycling through the night vision back to your regular eyesight. Let's try to hurry and not make this an all-day affair please," Mr. Rodriguez said, staring directly at Jericho.

Once everyone had cycled through and got back to seeing the world for what it was they grabbed up their bags and looked towards JJ's father for further instructions. He willingly provided them.

"Follow me. Don't lollygag. Watch your surroundings," he blandly instructed.

After he finished his brief instructions Mr. Rodriguez started down a long hallway and the others didn't hesitate to follow. He led them down countless hallways and through many doors. After what felt like minutes of walking through a labyrinth of hallways in dead silence they arrived at a large pair of double doors. There was a plaque above the doors that read 'Elemental Training Area'. Mr. Rodriguez pushed the doors inwards and then proceeded into the room. Once the doors had slammed shut behind them and everyone put their bags down, Mr. Rodriguez addressed them.

"Children, this is our Elemental Training Facility. As I'm sure you all heard AVA say, she's monitoring everyone's biometrics as she does with all who enter. If anything were to shift drastically, like a sudden spike or drop in temperature, she'd alert us immediately. So in other words you are in almost no safer place than here. I guarantee you. We have something else to take care of before you get fully acquainted with the training facility. Follow me to the conjoining room because if I'm not mistaken your Core Symbols will be appearing any minute now. We spent a lot more time in the desert than I thought we would. C'mon now," he directed them.

They followed Mr. Rodriguez to a small connecting room and no sooner had they crossed the threshold, Cindy let out a horrific shriek. She collapsed to the floor and the others stared in horror as they watched her skin sizzle. Within the next agonizing minute, the Core Symbol for Earth had been branded into Cindy's left forearm.

Cindy stared at her Core Symbol glowing in her skin and winced. She touched her arm with two fingers and immediately regretted the choice. Her arm felt as if it had been dipped in a pool of lava and she screamed while tears cascaded down her cheeks. When the screaming had subsided and Cindy calmed down, Mr. Rodriguez spoke.

"Okay does anybody know who's next?" He asked, seemingly unmoved by Cindy's agony.

"I think it was JJ," Charlotte told him.

All eyes turned to JJ and his face lit up with fear. He didn't want to be the next to go through what looked to be some very excruciating pain.

"JJ," Cindy whispered and grabbed JJ's arm. "Brace yourself."

"No, no, no," JJ panicked. "I don't wanna be next."

"Calm down and take a seat," his dad told him, motioning to chairs nobody had noticed before.

Charlotte and Mr. Rodriguez got Cindy to her feet. They started to get her over to the chairs but when they all turned around they saw JJ faceplant into a chair then hit the floor. The whole way down he clenched his arm and grimaced in pain. JJ's burning flesh hissed as he writhed around on the floor, yelling out in pain. When his shouting stopped, he saw the Core Symbol for Fire glowing red in his arm.

"Are you okay?" JJ's dad asked him.

"You said it would hurt *slightly*," he replied. "That was way more than slightly."

"So yes?"

"Yes," JJ grunted.

Everyone except for Mr. Rodriguez was now seated and patiently awaiting the Symbols' next victim. Moments of dead silence passed between them before Charlotte and Jericho shared an outburst of agony. Cindy held Charlotte's hand as she screamed through the process. JJ locked eyes with Jericho and firmly grasped the arm that was being etched in glowing white. When the screams had passed Jericho looked exhausted and his face was drained of color but he managed to look down at his Symbol.

"Thanks for breaking my hand," Cindy said to Charlotte sarcastically.

"Any day of the week," she said back. She lifted her arm and saw the radiant blue Symbol that was now burned into her.

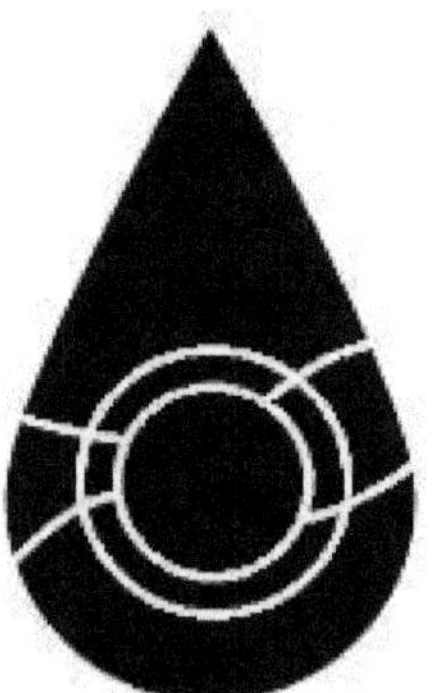

"Just like the Cores," Charlotte said as she stared in wonderment. "Super freaking beautiful."

"Agreed," Jericho said.

"Where's my dad?" JJ asked loudly, looking around.

The four exchanged unknowing glances and shrugs before Mr. Rodriguez called to them.

"I'm out here!" He called from the training area. "C'mon we've got work to do!"

They all walked out into the training area and gathered behind JJ's dad, who was pressing buttons on a holographic wall panel that was making various beeping sounds. He finished and turned around to face them.

"Sooo," he started, "Cinthya, you've used to your Core Powers already correct?" He asked, already knowing the answer.

"Yes sir," she replied proudly.

"And just you?" He directed the question at everybody.

"No sir," Jericho said, "I used my Powers also. Nowhere close to the magnitude that Cindy used hers, but still."

When?" Mr. Rodriguez asked.

"Yesterday after, no before, Zach bonded with the Magma Core," he responded.

"Alright then Ms. Thompson, you're first up to use your Powers. Go ahead and stand over there on the silver platform and await further instructions while everyone else stays on this side of the room with me. Mr. Umpter, you're on deck. We'll start there for now," Mr. Rodriguez finished.

JJ's dad pressed a button on the panel and the floor separated, revealing the top of a large transparent wall that arose from the floor, separating Cindy from everyone else. Within twenty seconds the wall touched the ceiling and locked into place. He pressed another button and this time, the floor around Cindy opened up and an array of rocks, boulders, and rubble lifted up from underneath the floor. She stood there quietly waiting to find out what would happen next, as did all of the others. Once everything had settled into place, Mr. Rodriguez pressed the intercom button on the wall panel. When he spoke, his voice came out of speakers built into the room all around Cindy.

"Ms. Thompson, can you hear me?" He asked.

"Yes sir," she replied. "Can you hear me?

Mr. Rodriguez chuckled to himself and said, "Yes we can. Loud and clear. Alright," he continued, "can you remember the feeling of emotion you experienced when you used your Powers?"

"I guess."

"Cinthya, you need to remember. It's vital to making the connection and accessing your Powers," he told her. "Can you remember?" He repeated.
Cindy closed her eyes and tried to recall the feelings from two days prior.

After a brief moment of hard thinking, she opened her eyes and said, "I remember."

"Excellent! Now try to connect with the Earth Elemental by remembering that feeling. Let it wash over you and fill you up to the point where you feel as if you'll overflow. Then, once you establish the connection you can try moving the smaller rocks, boulders, or anything else there," he instructed. "Whenever you're ready," he assured her in a calming voice.

Slowly the memory replayed into her mind as she closed her eyes and recollected the exact moment she had first used her Powers.

She saw JJ trapped under the enormous rock that wedged itself above him. Charlotte and Jericho were beside her pushing the boulder as hard as they could but to no avail. She saw her friends' faces awash with concern as she ranted about their precarious situation. Then she saw the Terra Core in her hand, radiating beauty as always. That warm adrenaline feeling crept back into her body and her fingertips started to tingle. *She saw darkness,* and the feeling intensified and started boiling up inside of her, spreading throughout and warming her insides. *The darkness disappeared and she was staring directly at the boulder above her friend.* Her heart began to race, the thumping in her chest made it feel as if she were free falling. Butterflies swarmed in her stomach, fluttering excitedly. *She backed away from the boulder, ran up close to it, and pushed her arms forward, willing the boulder away from her and her friends.* Her heart stampeded in her chest and she felt as if she was going to burst any second.

"Warning!" AVA alerted them in an alarming tone. "Cinthya Thompson's heart rate is reaching an alarmingly high level!"

"Everything's fine!" Mr. Rodriguez called back.

"One hundred bpm and climbing!" AVA warned.

"I have it under control!" He insisted loudly.

"Understood," AVA said and went silent.

As Cindy stood there over-energized and bubbling with power, a smile spread across her lips. The power she felt dwindled for a split second before she squeezed her eyes shut even tighter and let out a loud, forceful grunt as she threw her hands up into the air. She could feel the power now heavily condensed in her hands as she stood there with her eyes shut, firmly holding her position. She barely heard Charlotte's voice over the sound of her heart beating.

"No freaking way!" She shouted. "Girl, open your eyes!"

Cindy did as her friend said and couldn't believe what she saw when her eyelids lifted. Every single piece of rock that had come from under the floor was now floating throughout the air. She moved her arms up and down which caused the rocks to bob up and down midair. A huge grin spread across her face.

Hello, a voice said to Cindy in her mind.

Uh, hi. Are you-, Cindy started to ask.

-The Earth Elemental? The one and only, The Earth Elemental introduced itself.

Nice to meet you, I guess.

You as well.

"Do you see it Uncle Anthony?! I'm doing it!" She yelled.

"I see, you're doing very well, Cinthya. Now try setting them down nice and ea-," he said before Cindy dropped her hands and all of the rocks crashed into the floor.

"My bad," she apologized.

It happens to the best of us, Earth told her.

"It's alright. How do you feel?" He asked.

"Honestly I feel great," she told him.

"Do you hear the Earth Elemental?"

"Yeah. It's kind of strange."

"I'd assume so."

"Are my eyes all glowy like yours are?"

"Indeed they are. It looks kind of-," he started but was interrupted by his son.
"-Super freaking awesome!" JJ yelled.

"Awesome," Cindy repeated, incredibly proud of herself.

Mr. Rodriguez called out to the building's AI. "Run Cinthya's vitals," he ordered.

"Running vital analysis. One moment please," AVA's voice answered. A few seconds passed before AVA spoke again. "Analysis complete. Vitals are steady."

"Thank you," Mr. Rodriguez said.

"Cinthya, you're welcome to try out your Powers for a few minutes to get used to them."

"Roger that," she said.

Cindy let that familiar sensation come over her again and she stared down the biggest boulder. She focused the energy into her hands before putting them out in front of her and raising them up slowly, causing the boulder to ascend.

Feels good doesn't it? Earth asked rhetorically.

It feels all warm and comforting, Cindy answered.

I see what you want to do.

Wait, so you can see my thoughts as they're forming.

Yup. So be careful, okay?

I will. I promise.

"This actually isn't that hard," she told everyone.

She kept her left hand steady as she moved her right hand away and raised another boulder into the air.

"I'm gonna try something," she told Mr. Rodriguez.

"Be careful. You can't feel them now, but your body has limitations. If you overexert yourself now, there will be negative consequences," he warned.

"I'll be careful," she insisted.

She closed her eyes and started bringing her hands closer together putting the boulders on a collision course.

You really got the hang of this, Earth noted.

Thank you, Cindy said.

My energy's in your hands now. Give 'em a show.

She willed more power into her hands after Earth's ego boost. She felt like she was getting adjusted to the sensation of the Elemental's energy flowing through her, so she continued to bring them even closer. They were just a few feet away from colliding when Cindy released a deep, booming scream. Her hands clapped together and she watched the two boulders crash and merge together, making a deformed blocky sideways number eight.

Jericho said, "whoa," and Cindy looked over at him with pride illuminating her face.

"Oh yeah, but I ain't done yet," she said confidently and turned back around to face her creation.

Cindy held the rock steady with her left hand and slashed the air sideways in front of her with her right. The rock made a loud crunching noise and began to crack. A large chunk fell from the bottom and hit the floor loudly, leaving a straight edge. Again she slashed the air causing the rock to crunch and crack but nothing fell from it. Slowly she lowered her hand and the rock from the air. When the rock was a few feet from the floor she rotated her hand causing a huge slab of the boulder to slide off of the top, leaving a parallel straight edge. As carefully as she could, she set the flattened rock on the floor and walked over to it.

"What are you doing?" Charlotte asked.

"Just watch and see," Cindy insisted.

Do you think this is a good idea? Cindy asked Earth.

I think that, if done correctly, it will have interesting results, Earth responded.

So it'll be fun?

More than likely.

That's good enough for me.

Earth chuckled in her mind. ***Thought it would be.***

Cindy climbed on top of the flat rock and spread her arms to resemble a surfer riding a wave. She raised both of her arms into the air and the rock began to rise up from the floor beneath her. Within seconds she was three feet in the air riding her rock hoverboard. She guided it around the room with her fists clenched in front of her like a superhero.

"This is totally wicked!" She yelled soaring past the transparent wall.

"And dangerous," Mr. Rodriguez mumbled.

"Lighten up dad," JJ said. "She's just having fun."
"I understand that but she's not the least bit concerned about her safety," his dad told him.

"You want me to stop?" Cindy asked him. "By the way you're standing right by the mic."

Earth's voice spoke through Cindy's mouth.

"Oh Anthony," The Elemental said. "Are you still a party pooper? Light."

"Earth. How are you?" Mr. Rodriguez asked, ignoring the rude insinuation.

"Fine. My Elementalist is very free spirited. I like her."

"I'm sure. I'd like to speak with her if you please."

Earth buried itself back into Cindy's mind and allowed Cindy to speak for herself.

"Please lower yourself back down to the floor," Mr. Rodriguez said.

"Okay," she said as she started to descend. "That was awesome. I can't wait to try that again," she said when she got off of the rock. "Safely of course," she added quickly.

"Of course," Mr. Rodriguez said, smiling.

He's still a party pooper, Earth told Cindy.

Kind of, but he's just a worrier, Cindy reassured.

I guess you're right.

Jericho exhaled heavily before nervously asking, "Do I really have to go next?"

"'Fraid so my boy," Mr. Rodriguez said after pressing the button that lowered the glass.

Cindy walked over to the group as Jericho walked away from them. He and Cindy met in between and she stopped him in his tracks to hug him.

"Don't worry," she whispered in his ear, "it's way easier to do than it looks. Your Elemental will do most of the work. Plus look at this."

She opened her hand and the Terra Core was resting in her palm.

"How?" Jericho asked her.

Cindy's eyes began to glow and the Earth Elemental spoke to him through her.

"I held onto it for her just as I'm certain Air is doing for you," the Earth Elemental told him.

Her eyes stopped glowing and Cindy had a strange look on her face.
"When Earth talks through me it feels like me but not me at the same time. You'll see," she told him, realizing how crazy of a sentence that was. "Anyway listen, I'm so sure you're gonna do great. Show 'em what you're made of Jay."

"You got it," he said as he walked past her towards the platform in the middle of the training area.

Once Cindy was on the side with the others, Mr. Rodriguez raised the glass and lowered the boulders. Two giant fans slowly rose up from under the floor on either side of Jericho.

"Mr. Umpter, it should be relatively easy to use your powers without assistance when you connect with Air, but, seeing as this is your first official time using your Core Powers, the fans can be turned on to help you if you want them," Mr. Rodriguez told him.

"Okay," was all Jericho said.

"Jericho, do you want me to turn them on?"

"No. I would, uh, like to try without them if that's cool."

"Alright then. Try to connect with the Air Elemental," he instructed.

Jericho closed his eyes and concentrated for what felt like hours.

"Are you good Jerry?" JJ asked through the speaker, cutting into his friend's poor attempt at concentration.

Jericho relaxed and told him, "Yeah I'm good."

"Dope. Dope."

"So, uh, how long has it been?" Jericho asked, picking up the awkwardness in JJ's response.

"How long?" JJ asked behind him. "Cindy says eight minutes, my guy."

"Dang," he whispered in response to the update. "Feels like eighty for real, for real," he told him.

"You need the fans or something?"

"Nah, but Cindy," he called.

"What's up?" She asked.

"Come here a sec, would ya?" Jericho asked back.

"Sure," she said and got up from her seat.

Mr. Rodriguez lowered the glass wall allowing Cindy to go over to Jericho. When she got to him, she could clearly see the frustration painted on his face.

"You good?" Cindy asked.

"Not really," Jericho confessed.

"Yeah. Looks like you're not really connecting with the Elemental."

"Guess Air isn't as willing as Earth."
"Not as easy for you as it was for me," she teased lightly.

"It's hard as fuck," he whispered.

"I heard that Jericho," Mr. Rodriguez called.

"Sorry Pops," Jericho called back. "How'd you do it?" He asked her.

"I focused on the memory I guess. Once I remembered how it happened the first time, this time was a cake walk."

"All I did was stop a Core from hitting the floor."

"Not really awe-inspiring motivation, huh?" she asked rhetorically. "How 'bout this? Don't worry about the connection, focus on the power. There's something inside of you that the Air Elemental thought made you the right choice to be Its Elementalist, you don't have to decide what it is."

"That was pretty good," he admitted.
"Thanks. Now, try focusing on a different strong memory. Uncle Anthony told us it's a strong emotional connection that triggers everything. You can do it," she told him and held up a fist.

He bumped her fist and whispered, "I can do this," to himself. Cindy walked back over to the group and once again the wall rose up to touch the ceiling. It locked in place, leaving Jericho isolated with his thoughts. Jericho closed his eyes and began searching for an emotionally charged memory.

The first one to come to mind was the day that his guardian, Stephanie, bought him his first car. She surprised him with it on his sixteenth birthday, hours after he found a card his mother had left him before she died. It was so nice and he was filled with a mixture of emotions ranging from gratitude to depression to happiness.

Nope, too regular. I mean eventually everybody gets a car, he thought to himself.

The next one he remembered was the day he'd won the national spelling bee and fell off of the stage when he got too excited. He laughed. *Not quite good enough*, he thought. Then he remembered the first time he met his best friend, JJ. The memory uncontrollably flooded his mind.

Stephanie was holding his hand as they stood outside of a house that he'd never seen before. He was so afraid that he was shaking.

"This is Justin and Mr. Rodriguez's house," she explained to him softly. "Wanna know something funny?" She asked him.

He nodded his head up and down slightly.

"I don't call him Mr. Rodriguez. I call him Pops."

Jericho giggled at the silly moniker.

"Okay now look Jay, Mr. Rodriguez was good friends with your mom a long time ago. He's super duper smart and he's really funny too. He's going to take you to daycare with his son Justin today, okay? They're super duper nice," she told him.

"You swear?" He asked her and held up his pinky.

"I swear," she said and smiled, wrapping her pinky around his.

Mr. Rodriguez opened the door, shook his hand like a grown up, and invited him in. Stephanie kissed him on his forehead and said she'd pick him up later from daycare.

"We're about to have breakfast," Mr. Rodriguez said. "Are you hungry?"

Jericho nodded quietly.

"Take a seat at the counter next to that big headed boy," Mr. Rodriguez told him.

"Daddy! My head's not that big!" JJ yelled.

He watched as Mr. Rodriguez laughed, went into the kitchen, and grabbed three bowls and spoons. He and JJ were sitting at JJ's kitchen counter waiting for Mr. Rodriguez to get the milk and cereal. Mr. Rodriguez placed two cereals on the counter in front of them, Lucky Charms and Frosted Flakes. Jericho reached out for the Lucky Charms but JJ intercepted them.

"It's your first day so I'm gonna go easy on you," JJ said to him, his voice unnecessarily confrontational. "You gotta earn Lucky Charms in this house. You want something, you earn it. Whether it's Lucky Charms or-," he was cut off.

"-Or someone's respect," JJ's father had said.

Jericho's mind snapped back to the present.

"Or the right to be the Turbulent Core Elementalist," he said in a hushed tone.

A pressure was building up inside of him until Jericho had no choice but to let it burst out. His whole body shot up from the floor and his ears popped. When he finally opened his glowing white eyes he saw Mr. Rodriguez and his friends staring up at him from across the room several feet below him. He looked down at his legs which were dangling beneath him and laughed at the sight of them.

"It's been sooo long," said a voice that wasn't Jericho's, but came from his mouth.
"Whoa!" Jericho yelled, startled by this new development. "Um, Air?"

"That's correct!" Air shouted.
"It's weird that we're both using my mouth."

"A little bit. You'll get used to it. So are you gonna let me make you look awesome or what?"

"I'm down for whatever."

"Excellent. You're in the driver seat and I'll supercharge the car."

"This is amazing!" Jericho yelled and willed the air around him to push him to the glass. "Turn on the fans."

"Aye, aye," Mr. Rodriguez said and pressed a big windmill button, turning on the fans.

The big metallic fans creaked to life and within seconds they were pumping air throughout Jericho's side of the room. With all of the air blowing around him, Jericho couldn't help but be overcome with an overwhelming sensation of invigoration. He directed the air into a wide current and made it push him all around the room.

"JJ, I can fly!" Jericho yelled to his best friend.

"Really?" He yelled back. "looks more like hovering to me," he jested. "Kidding, kidding. Show me what you're made of Jerry."

You got it, Jericho said in his head, and was surprised when the voice of Air said something in there as well.

Jericho, Air said.

Can you hear my thoughts? Jericho questioned the Elemental.

I picked you because of your intelligence. Don't make me regret it, Air told him.

I mean, I figured you could, Jericho said defensively.

Yet, you still asked the question.

It was semi-rhetorical. You're snippy, dude.

Don't call me dude. I'm eons older than you.

So what do I–

–Air.

Air? That's it? Never mind. Got it.

Let's do it!

Do what?

Jericho, I'm in your mind. I know what you wanna do.

Can I really do it?

Didn't the bearer of Light tell you that your Core Powers are exponential?

Yes. I mean he did but–

–So man up and stop being a little bitch.

Alright, let's do it. Wait, you cuss?

This isn't my first rodeo.

Apparently not.

The mental conversation ended and Jericho willed the air currents to not only push him, but also flow around him creating a tunnel-like current. He straightened his body making it parallel to the floor, and began to pick up speed.

Put your arms out in front of you to have more turning control as you pick up speed, Air advised him.

Jericho did as he was advised and began to pick up speed, willing the current to push him faster and faster around the room.

"Warning! Jericho Umpter's heart rate is accelerating at an alarming pace!" AVA warned, but Jericho couldn't even hear it because the whistling in his ears was roaring too loudly.

"Jericho stop!" Mr. Rodriguez demanded, but again, the whistling was too loud.

Jericho continued picking up speed. *Gotta go faster*, he thought.

I agree. We're very close.

Around and around the room he went as the group and AVA yelled inaudible warnings at him.

Almost there, Air whispered in Jericho's mind.

"Dad! Do something!" JJ pleaded.

"I'm thinking," Mr. Rodriguez told him. "Light?"

If something moves fast enough it fractures sound, Light said in Mr. Rodriguez's head.

"Oh no," Mr. Rodriguez said.

"Oh no, what?" Charlotte asked fearfully. "Oh no's are never good."

"He's trying to break the sou-," was all he could say before Jericho did what he set out to do.

A deafening boom exploded on Jericho's side of the room. Jericho shattered the sound barrier and caused a sonic boom. His body couldn't take the intensity of the blast and fell from the top of the room towards the floor.

"Bring the boulders back up and lower the glass," Cindy demanded.

Mr. Rodriguez unhesitatingly pressed a sequence of buttons that followed her commands. Cindy threw her hands out to sense the boulder and found it seconds before Jericho hit the floor.

Earth! Cindy shouted frantically in her head.

You need assistance? Earth asked.

Please.

As you wish.

Her eyes lit up and she slammed her left fist, knuckle down, into her right hand. Then she quickly raised it to the ceiling, causing the flattened rock to shoot up from under the floor. Just as soon as it looked as if the rock was going to collide with Jericho, Cindy closed her hand into a tight fist. The rock snapped over him before crashing into the floor.

"What the hell did you just do?" JJ asked Cindy threateningly.

"I just saved your best friend from becoming a stain on the floor," she snapped back.

The wall finally lowered enough to get over and everyone surged over to Cindy's rock.

"Where is he?" Charlotte asked.

"He's inside," Cindy grunted as she pried open her fist.

The rock opened up just like Cindy's hand and Jericho was safely inside. He had a cut on his forehead that looked to have been caused by the rock. JJ backed away from Jericho's unconscious body.

"AVA give me Jericho's heart rate. Now!" Mr. Rodriguez ordered.

"Jericho Umpter's heart rate has slowed to fifteen BPM, CPR should be performed immediately," AVA frantically informed them.

"I got it," Cindy said and swiped her hand downward and the rock flattened out. She pinched Jericho's nose, took a deep breath, and exhaled into his mouth. She did it again before she started pressing on his chest. When she got to the twelfth compression Jericho's eyes opened and he started coughing.

"He's okay," Cindy announced.

"AVA," Mr. Rodriguez said aloud.

"Heart rate returning to normal Sir," AVA said. "Fifty-six BPM and climbing."

Jericho stared at them talking but didn't say anything.

Did I die? He asked Air.

I'm pretty sure you didn't. A solid ninety-three percent sure, Air replied.

So there's a seven percent chance I kicked the bucket.

C'est la vie.

Bite me.

Mr. Rodriguez got him to his feet and asked him how he felt. Jericho tried to tell him but immediately started coughing again. Jericho nodded his head and mouthed, 'I feel like I got kicked by a horse.'
"You almost died," Mr. Rodriguez said quietly to Jericho. "I said your body has limitations but you won't be able to feel them in this state, remember?"

Jericho managed a weak nod.

Tell him you thought I could do it, Jericho said to Air.

Why, the heck, would I do that? Air asked quickly.

Because my body is too weak to do it.

So?

You said I could do it and I almost died. A lot of this is your fault.

Ooh. Can't argue there.

Jericho's eyes began to glow a radiant white and Air spoke to Mr. Rodriguez. "Anthony, Light, Jericho wanted me to tell you that I told him that I thought it would be okay to break the sound barrier," Air admitted.

Mr. Rodriguez's comforting look turned into a scowl and his eyes started to glow a burning yellow.

"Why would you do that, Air?" Asked Light's stern voice. "He's only but a child."

"Brother. He's my Elementalist," Air responded, "it was my decision."

"It was foolish."

"But-."

"-You exist to represent intelligence. Don't insult the Core Being by acting impetuously and making silly unjustified decisions. Understand?"

"You have to realize-."

"-Do you understand?!" Light shouted the question.

"Yes brother," Air surrendered.

Mr. Rodriguez and Jericho returned back to themselves. "That's gonna take some getting used to," Jericho told Mr. Rodriguez.

"You don't get used to it," Mr. Rodriguez told Jericho. "You just suck it up and let it happen.

"I guess I'll find out for myself."

"The sonic boom was impressive though. Well done Mr. Umpter, well done."

Jericho smiled.

"Dad," JJ said loudly, making everyone divert their attention to him.

His dad and Jericho turned around and saw his face flushed and full of concern. Mr. Rodriguez ushered the others into the safety zone as his son's face continued to redden. JJ felt the air become uncomfortably dry and his lips chap up as he stared at the others. Sweat dripped from behind his ears, running down his neck and into his shirt. His clothes spontaneously burst into flames, causing fear to jump into his voice.

"Nobody else's clothes burned off!" He shouted to the group who were now behind the glass wall.

"You will be fine Justin," his dad reassured him, "just stay calm and you WILL be fine."

"My, m-my eyes hurt," JJ stuttered as he placed his hands on his eyes.

"How are they hurting?"

"They burn dad! They burn!" He screamed, revealing his eyes which were glowing an intense burning red.

JJ stopped screaming and stood dead silent facing the glass, his clothes continuing to burn around him.

"JJ," Charlotte said quietly.

A grimace spread across his face seconds before he erupted in an enormous mass of fire, making everyone else avert their eyes. They looked up to see a giant cyclops made of fire looming before them behind the glass. It had two curved horns on the top of its head and its giant eye was sealed tight. The giant's nose was identical to JJ's, including the scar leading diagonally from his right nostril onto his cheek. The cyclops opened its eye and revealed a piercing red iris encircled by a glowing white pupil. The fiery eye blinked once and the cyclops smiled at everyone.

"Had to show everybody what Fire was made of. My Elementalist is strong," the deep voiced cyclops known as Fire boasted.

Mr. Rodriguez' eyes instantly lit back up.

"You're going to kill him before his journey can begin," Light spoke angrily through Mr. Rodriguez.

"Light! How are you?" Fire asked, completely bypassing the grim news.

"Release your true form!" Light demanded. "Your Elementalist will die otherwise!"

"He's fine," Fire told Light assuringly.

"Release your true form, you cocky bastard!" Mr. Rodriguez screamed. "I won't tell you again!"

"Nor will I," Light added in an incredibly serious tone.

The cyclops gave a grimace and a final blink before all of the fire dissipated, leaving JJ standing in its place, pale and exposed. JJ was totally deafened by the experience so he couldn't hear when his father walked over to him but he could see him speaking. His dad helped him into the pair of shorts from his duffel and guided him back to the safety zone. Cindy opened her mouth to speak once the two Rodriguezes sat down, but Mr. Rodriguez halted her.

"It's called Titan Form. Every Elementalist can *eventually* develop the ability to literally switch physical forms and morph into the true form of their Elemental, but it takes an immense amount of power. Not to mention," he paused and looked at his son who he was helping shakily put on a T-shirt, "the physical toll on the Elementalist. Bottom line is, don't even THINK about attempting something of that magnitude because none of you are even close to being close to being ready."

After a few seconds, Cindy just couldn't help herself.

"So can you, uh, turn into a Titan?" Cindy asked.

JJ's dad shot her a look of annoyance mixed heavily with anger.

"I can, but I won't."

"So," Charlotte said after a brief moment of awkward silence, "I'm supposed to follow up that spectacle, am I? Well, let's see what I can do."

She strode out into the training area and waited for the glass wall to rise once again. Mr. Rodriguez pressed an array of buttons that caused the floor to slide away around her and in their place, large open tanks of water replaced them. *A powerful memory,* Cindy had told Jericho. Charlotte closed her eyes and was instantaneously drowned in emotional memories. One memory overpowered the others and she was dragged into darkness. *She was seven again.*

"Charlotte!" Her mother screamed so loudly that Charlotte had been able to hear it underwater.

Slowly Charlotte sank, lower and lower. Out of breath. Out of time. She was exhausted after trying to resurface and could only watch as the bright blue world turned black. Her arms floating above her as she continued to descend. Her eyelids became heavy and the darkness was overwhelming. Almost inviting. She closed her eyes and it was abnormally bright again. A giant white light shone bright in the distance, beckoning her to come close to it. She moved closer and closer to the light and began to feel safe. It had a familiar warmth that was impossible to resist. It sang to her a soft, sweet song that flowed through her, promising release. Once she was right upon it, she reached out to touch it and was yanked down the path she came. She opened her eyes to blinding sunlight, leaned over, and vomited seawater onto the beach. She could hear muffled cheering all around her and saw her mother in her father's arms, crying and smiling. They walked over and thanked a kneeling lifeguard before her father scooped her up and took her back to their car.

Charlotte opened her eyes and was shocked to see a visual representation, constructed out of water, of her father carrying her to the car walking alongside her mother. Tears were rolling down her cheeks and she welcomed them. She dropped her hands and the watery image deconstructed and splashed around her.

"Light," a voice that wasn't Charlotte's said before her eyes stopped glowing.

"Letty. You okay?" Cindy asked her in a cautious tone.

"Yeah. Yeah Cee Cee, I'm fine," Charlotte answered softly. "How'd I do? I mean, that was no Titan, sonic boom, or rock hoverboard."
"You did magnificent, Ms. Santiago," Mr. Rodriguez told her and smiled.

"Good to know," Charlotte told him and smiled back.

Charlotte rejoined the group and took a seat next to JJ. He looked up from the floor where he'd been staring and saw her looking at him with a sad but gentle expression.

"You okay?" She asked him.

"Yeah, I, uh, ate a banana," he told her and laughed, slightly embarrassed. "Plus I drank some Powerade while you were, uh, yeah," he trailed off. "Charlie."

"Yeah?"

"Are *you* okay?"

"Well. It turns out rocks give people superpowers and my friends and I found one and got the other. JJ, I'm better than I ever thought possible," she told him with a small smile creasing her lips.

"Good to know," he said, smiling back.

"On to the next task children," Mr. Rodriguez announced. "Follow me."

3:45 PM
Combat Training Area

Everyone followed Mr. Rodriguez through two hallways and into a room that looked similar to the Elemental Training Area. Although, in this room spacious racks lined the far walls holding an array of bow staffs, fencing foils, épées, and sabers along with protective equipment in various body sizes. They filtered into the room and began observing the whole of the combat training area. Four large black plates covered sections of the floor, and a path was marked on the floor showing you where you could walk. Mr. Rodriguez walked over to another holographic wall panel, similar to the one in the previous room. He pressed on numerous buttons and spoke to the others over his shoulder.

"Those bulky panels you see on the floor are practice areas. The four holographic projectors on the four corners of each panel can display a variety of different arenas. A boxing ring, wrestling mats, deserts, forests, buildings," Mr. Rodriguez trailed off. He picked his train of thought back up and continued, "Those are just a few off of the top of my head. Anyway, in this training area you will learn basic combat skills for a multitude of scenarios. So if someone wants to hurt you and you want to dodge, reverse, and make them hurt themselves, you can. Someone pulls a gun on you and you need to disarm them, you can. You need to incapacitate someone for exactly twelve minutes, you can. Bottom line, you're going to become badasses. Now, the floor uses 'Pop-Touch Technique' to simulate the floor of the arena underfoot, making the training more realistic. Take your duffels into the locker rooms," he paused and pointed to doors on the far right wall, "and get changed. Meet me back here in ten minutes. Break!"

The four of them walked into the locker rooms, changed, and headed back out to the training area. Mr. Rodriguez had changed into a T-shirt and basketball shorts identical to the ones the others changed into. He'd also taken off his shoes and directed the other to do the same. He gave Cindy and Charlotte hair ties and they put their hair up, awaiting further instructions.
"Excelente, now if you all wouldn't mind standing in the middle of that panel there, we can get started."

They walked over to the panel and stepped on. It was cold and bumpy under their feet so they found themselves shuffling around impatiently waiting for the next task. Mr. Rodriguez pressed a big button on the wall panel causing the holographic projectors to hum to life, causing the whole floor to be replaced by a convincing replica of wrestling mats. Mr. Rodriguez jogged over and stepped onto the mat. All at once the floor buzzed underneath everyone's feet.

"What's going on?" Charlotte asked.

"It's measuring you," Mr. Rodriguez told her.

"Measuring? What does that mean?"

"The floor is recording your weight and the size of your feet so it knows where to pop-touch you and how hard. Every step you take gets pop-touched individually so that it can feel more realistic for each person."

When he finished explaining, he began stretching, which confused everyone else. They waited for his next direction and it didn't come. He just closed his eyes and continued stretching. Slowly they caught on and began stretching as well.

"Why are we stretching?" JJ asked.
"This exercise will be exhausting and your Elementals won't help you handle this challenge," his dad answered.

"Which is?"

"You will have to work as a team to defeat me."

JJ stifled a laugh and said, "You? C'mon you can't be serious."

"Oh, but I am. Don't think of me as much of a challenge, my boy?"

"No. Not really."

"Do you all agree? Mr. Rodriguez asked the others.
The three of them told him that they agreed.

"Interesting. Well who first then to go against me, seeing as though I'm not a challenge?"

JJ stepped forward and the floor felt slick beneath his feet. "What are the rules?" He asked.

"They go as follows. You fall, you lose. Use whatever technique you need to knock over the opponent. Before we start you'll need protective gear."

"I think I'll be fine," JJ said confidently.

"Suit yourself. Gimme your best shot."

JJ approached his father and got into a crouched wrestling stance. He started circling his father who played along and started walking in circles as well. With every step the floor slicked and sank beneath JJ's feet. He lunged forward and got low in an attempt to grapple his dad, but his dad reacted so quickly that JJ couldn't believe his eyes. His dad vaulted over him and landed behind him with a THUD. He swept kicked his son's legs out from under him and he fell forward. JJ hit the floor, face first, and just lied there for a second, sprawled out and defeated. His dad walked over to and helped him up from off of the floor.

"Not what you were expecting, was it?" His dad asked sarcastically.

"Nope. Not one bit," he responded. "So we're probably gonna need that gear."

"Yeah, I'd say so."

The two of them walked over to the others, who'd stepped off the practice area when the match first started.

"So who's next?" Mr. Rodriguez asked.

"JJ. Sidebar, now," Cindy said ignoring the question and pulling JJ away from his dad and into a group huddle. "Two words. Bad. Ass. Your dad is a freaking monster.
"I have to agree," JJ told her. "We've severely underestimated him."

"You think? He put you on your ass before any of us even saw it coming," Jericho chimed in.

"I sure did," Mr. Rodriguez said, suddenly standing right behind them. "Is everything alright?"

"No," Charlotte told him. "You are an extremely good fighter and, no offense, you're like, a dad. What gives?"

"Combat is about moves and countermoves, just like chess. If you only focus on what your opponent is doing now then you'll be unprepared for the move they're about to do next. Like between JJ and I, I saw he was looking at my legs before we started circling. I anticipated he would grapple, which he did, so I made sure to get ahead of the move, jump over him, and sweep his legs from under him. Then I did, as you all just saw."

"Wow," Jericho said, astonished. You're like Robert Downey Jr. in Sherlock Holmes."

"I never thought of myself like that," he said and smiled. "Thank you."

"Great. Now you've boosted his ego," JJ told Jericho.

"Who's next?" Mr. Rodriguez asked again.
"Maybe we all work as a team and take you down," Charlotte suggested.

"I like the way your brain works Ms. Santiago," Mr. Rodriguez told her. "Let's get you in some gear and give it a go."

The four got equipped with safety gear and re-entered the practice area Mr. Rodriguez. He smiled at them and took his stance. They all followed suit and within moments, Mr. Rodriguez was surrounded by his opponents. JJ, Charlotte, Jericho, and Cindy began circling JJ's dad in unison, like vultures circling a carcass. Although he was outnumbered, Mr. Rodriguez was calm and collected. He rotated slowly in the opposite direction of the others and studied them all carefully.

His son had again taken a low wrestling crouch while, to his right, Jericho had both of his arms tucked into his sides at ninety-degree angles, a classic Taekwondo stance. Cindy had her right arm tucked at her side and her left extended toward him in a different Taekwondo stance. Charlotte held her hands up near her face and chest, a basic street fighting technique, although she also practiced wrestling and took the same two years of Taekwondo the others had.

JJ made a sound like 'tss-tss' and all at once, the four of them charged at his father. Charlotte was the first upon him and wasted no time. She threw a hard right jab towards his left shoulder. He sidestepped quickly and avoided the punch with ease before thrusting a flat palm into her chest, pushing her away from the fight. He immediately ducked and felt the air from Jericho's jumping spinning roundhouse kick and heard him land firmly behind him. Mr. Rodriguez whirled his neck to the right and saw his son coming in for the grapple. *Not this time,* he thought to himself before throwing all of his body weight into a backwards somersault. He felt his son's hand touch his leg in a pathetic attempt to grab him. He sprung to his feet and felt arms wrap around his torso.

"I really hope that you don't think that you are going to suplex me," Mr. Rodriguez said to the person holding him in their clutches.
"Actually that was the plan," Jericho responded.

"Just do it and stop talking!" JJ yelled, but it was too late.

Mr. Rodriguez broke free of Jericho's grasp and in the following few seconds, Jericho had been gut checked and knocked to the floor gasping for air.

"And then there were three," Mr. Rodriguez said ominously.

"Jerry, you good?" JJ asked, ignoring his father.

Jericho put a thumbs-up in the air and crawled off of the practice area. He curled up into the fetal position and layed perfectly still.

"That was a little aggressive, don't you think?" Charlotte asked.

"They won't be kind when they attack," Mr. Rodriguez said quickly.

"Who won't?" She asked, just as quickly.

Mr. Rodriguez swatted the question away and said, "For now, let's just train."

Cindy happily complied and jumped right into action, throwing a low left hook that nailed Mr. Rodriguez right in his side. He smiled at her in a weird way that made her feel slightly uncomfortable.

"Very good. You're the first one to land a strike," Mr. Rodriguez congratulated. Then his eyes hardened and he asked, "Can you dodge them as well?"

Mr. Rodriguez threw a barrage of combos at Cindy which she did her best to block, avoid, and return. A few of her blows landed but many more returned in their place. JJ and Charlotte rushed to her aid but just as they came within striking distance, a hard jab struck her left shoulder and she spiraled to the floor. Charlotte scrambled to her side and JJ put his father in a choke hold.

"Are you okay girl?" Charlotte asked Cindy.

"Yup. Maybe a little bruised but nothing an ice pack and rest won't fix," she told her.

"This is a good grip, I'll give you that much," Mr. Rodriguez told his son.

"I feel like there's a but," JJ said back.

"Ha, ha! Butt!" Jericho moaned loudly from somewhere behind them.

"Shut up idiot!" JJ called over his shoulder.

"But it's not enough to make me submit, so you'll lose," his dad explained.

"Not today. I'm gonna kamikaze," he told his dad as he kicked out their feet from under them and they fell backwards.

They crashed to the floor, breaking the hold and Mr. Rodriguez started laughing.

"You didn't have to say, *I'm gonna kamikaze*," Mr. Rodriguez told him. "You could've said something like, *I'm gonna sacrifice myself* or *I'm gonna take one for the team.* You are a piece of work boy."

"Can't argue there," JJ agreed and laughed.

"Good job everybody," Mr. Rodriguez praised them. "You all did excellent. Justin, what's that thing you say about teamwork and dreams?"

"Uh, teamwork makes the dream work," he pitched.

"Yes, that's the one. Keep working like that and you'll have nothing to fear."

What would we have to fear?" Jericho asked, still holding his stomach.

Mr. Rodriguez winced, realizing what he'd just done again. He indirectly mentioned the enemy.

That's twice in a matter of minutes. You'll have to tell them now, Light told him.

I know, Anthony responded quietly. *I know.*

"Get changed and-," Mr. Rodriguez started.

"-but what about Jericho's-," JJ interrupted.

"-JUST GO CHANGE JUSTIN!" Mr. Rodriguez yelled, silencing his son. "Then come out here so I can show you exactly what you have to fear," he instructed.

"Alright. Come on JJ," Jericho said, gently pushing his friend toward the locker room. "Charlotte and Cindy," he called, and waited for them to look up, "five minutes. Got it."

They both nodded and headed for the locker room, taking off pieces of padding as they went. JJ and Jericho followed their lead, leaving a trail of equipment in their wake.

4:45 PM
The Offices

The four of them followed behind JJ's dad without him uttering a sound. He led them down an infinite amount of lefts and rights, past numerous entryways, and eventually into a large office space. Mr. Rodriguez sat down at a dark brown desk and powered on the desktop computer and monitor. The screen blinked to life and awaited a password. Mr. Rodriguez raised his hands to the keyboard, where they hovered for moments.

"Could you please look away, all of you?" He asked softly.

"Dad, are you okay?" JJ asked.

His father's eyes began to glow and he snapped his fingers loudly. JJ, Jericho, Charlotte, and Cindy tried not to panic at the sudden condition of being completely blinded. Mr. Rodriguez typed his password into the computer.

P-A-M-E-L-A-S-C-O-T-T-R-O-D-R-I-G-U-E-Z – ENTER

His desktop screen appeared in front of him and he snapped his fingers again, giving everyone their vision back. With the newly reacquired vision they watched JJ's dad open a desktop folder titled 'Shadow Beasts' filled with dozens of jpg files. He got up from his computer and motioned for them to have a closer look at the folder's contents. JJ sat down in the chair and his friends huddled around him. He cautiously clicked on the first file, unsure and fearful of what they'd see. A picture of a weathered newspaper clipping from the late 1800's appeared in front of them entitled, 'Local Crazy Man Raves About Monsters.'

JJ read it aloud, "Victoria Walters claims that her husband, Archibald Walters, disappeared into the woods for eight days before returning in a delirious state. Archibald claims to have seen 'living shadows' in the forms of various monsters. He said he watched them for hours before being snuck up on by a smaller monster that scratched him up and forced him away. He then wandered around the woods for several days before finding his way back home and spreading the news to anyone who would lend an ear," he finished.

"Okay, so we're supposed to be scared of some shadow monsters?" Charlotte asked jokingly.
"Yeah," JJ agreed. "This article says dude was crazy sooo..." He trailed off.

Cindy exhaled heavily and then she spoke. "I hate to be *that guy* but, uh, does it really seem that far-fetched considering the amazing display of abilities that happened a little while ago in the Elemental Training Area? We were controlling elements people! Get a grip!" She finished.

"Actually, when you put it like that it does seem feasible that shadows could be morphed into monsters if there were an Elementalist to control them," Jericho concluded.

"Very true," Mr. Rodriguez agreed. "But these beasts, they don't need to be controlled."

"What?" They asked in a collective unison.

"The Shadow Beasts are physical manifestations of Chaos. If there is a living Mayhem Core Elementalist then the beasts will obey and do their bidding. On the other hand, if there isn't a living Mayhem Core Elementalist then the beasts have no one to answer to and follow the natural order. They are free to roam the Earth, terrorizing and killing innocent people. They destroy buildings and make disastrous events occur. They can be anywhere anytime, as long as there is a shadow to hide in. They live to fulfill the only goal they've ever been tasked with. Spreading Chaos. That's their true purpose."

A thick silence spread across the room. The four of them were absorbing the grim information that JJ's dad had begrudgingly provided. JJ turned back to the computer and clicked on the next file. Another detailed account of a person claiming to have seen shadow monsters. As he continued clicking through file after file and seeing article after article, he came upon a digitized picture of a woman. She had a pointed face and a rounded nose. Her skin was the shade of chocolate pudding and her eyes were blacker than death. A mess of scraggly brown hair enveloped her face and her teeth were yellow and just as crooked as her nose. She was truly hideous.

"Who is this woman?" JJ asked his dad.
"She was, as far as we know, the first Mayhem Core Elementalist to exist within this century. As for her name, that is unknown, as well as who she was, where she'd come from, how long she'd had her powers, and how much she knew about the Cores," Mr. Rodriguez explained.

"She was a horrific being," Fire said aloud, startling everyone.

"Fire, you knew her?" Charlotte asked, staring into JJ's glowing eyes.

"No I-," Fire started.

"-Then how do you know-," Cindy interjected.

"-I killed her," Fire finished, cutting her question short. "Well, my previous Elementalist-."

"-Fire," Mr. Rodriguez interrupted.

"I know the agreement Anthony. My previous Elementalist was incredibly strong and developed our bond and her abilities to a level she called Phoenix. This was when I learned that our true forms could be altered from Elementalist to Elementalist depending on how strongly they could strengthen their abilities," Fire finished.

"What do you mean?" Jericho asked.

"The Titan Transformation made me appear bird-like rather than my normal cyclopean form."

"Wow," Charlotte whispered.

JJ's eyes stopped glowing. "Man, that's a weird sensation," he said.

"Tell me about it," Jericho and Mr. Rodriguez said at the same.

JJ, Cindy, Charlotte, and Jericho turned around and stared at the woman's face for a few minutes. This woman had been known as the embodiment of Chaos and she looked the part. The longer they stared at the picture, the more haggard her face seemed to look. JJ clicked over to the next file and it was a hand drawn picture of a Shadow Beast that was signed 'P.S.'. The beast had teeth like knives and claws as long and sharp as katana blades. It stood on four broad legs and resembled a cross between a Rottweiler and a grizzly bear. Upon its back was what looked to be the woman in the previous picture. The woman and the beast were truly terrifying.

That's enough for now," Mr. Rodriguez told them. "Let's get you all something to eat and on your way to bed."

Nobody complained and followed JJ's dad out of the office, back through the infinite hallways, and finally into the mess hall. Apparently he had been coming there often and kept a deep freezer stocked with frozen pizzas and French fries. Once everyone had their food heated up and sat down to eat, a dozen questions spilled onto the table.

"Why do our eyes glow when we use our powers?" Charlotte asked.

"How soon until I can be a giant Earth Titan?" Cindy followed.

"Charlotte, I think it's because the Elementals are closer to the surface of, us?" he offered.

"Although I do know that only other Elementalists can see our auras. Also, I'm honestly not a hundred percent sure and Cinthya, like I said, it takes a lot of energy to transform into a titan so if you try before you're ready," he paused, "just don't try before you're ready."

"Are there any abilities that are similar between all of the Elementalists?" Jericho asked.

That's a good question, Air told him.

Thanks, Jericho said. ***Does it have a good answer?***

Yup. Listen closely.

"Well, I suppose the way we travel is similar," Mr. Rodriguez told him.
"How do you mean?"

"Well, I could just show you then explain if you'd like."

"Heck yeah!" Cindy yelled.

Everyone turned their gaze onto her.

"Sorry but this guy knows what he's doing and never fails to disappoint."
"That's true," Charlotte agreed.

"Alright dad, let's see it," JJ said.

Mr. Rodriguez wiped his mouth and got up from the table. He concentrated for a few seconds and his eyes ignited into that vibrant neon yellow.
"So are you gonna run or what?" Jericho asked.

"Shhh-ut up," Cindy demanded.

They stared at JJ's dad waiting for something to happen and then he just disappeared in a wisp of yellow light.

"Where the heck did he just go?" Jericho asked JJ.

"I-I don't know," JJ stuttered his answer.

"Mr. Rodriguez," Charlotte called out in a sing-song voice, "you in here?"

There was no reply.

"Do you Elementals know where he is?" Jericho asked, directing the question to Air, Earth, Fire, and Water.

At once, all of their eyes glowed and all of the Elementals spoke using their mouths.

"Of course," they all said.

"Can you tell us?" Charlotte asked in her own voice.

"No," Air said. "This is a very teachable moment. I still don't think you all quite grasp the scope of our power."

"Of course it is," Jericho retorted with the same mouth.

Their eyes returned to normal and they regained their composure.

"Maybe he's invisible," Cindy suggested.

"If that were the case, why wouldn't he say-," JJ started, but trailed off when his cell phone started ringing. "Holy shit," he said as he checked his phone.

"What're you so amped up about?" Jericho asked.
JJ turned his phone around and the others gasped at the picture on the screen. JJ's dad was posing in front of the Sphinx on the Giza Plateau in Egypt.

"Holy shit," JJ repeated.

"Watch your mouth Justin," Mr. Rodriguez warned his son.

Jericho turned around and yelped, surprised to see JJ's dad standing behind them.

"Holy shit!" He yelled.

"Really? You too?" Mr. Rodriguez asked rhetorically. "Do you girls need to yell holy shit along with these knuckleheads?"

"Sorry Pops," Jericho apologized.

"No I'm actually okay," Charlotte insisted.
"And I think I'll save mine for a more deserving occasion," Cindy decided.

"Wise choices," Mr. Rodriguez said to them. "Did you enjoy the photo?"

"Were you really-" Charlotte started.

"-Just in Egypt?" He finished her question.
"Yeah."

"Indeed I was, Ms. Santiago. Indeed I was," he answered dropping a handful of sand onto the table. "Question: How fast is the speed of light?"

"Isn't it like one hundred eighty-something thousand miles per second?" JJ asked.

"Six," Charlotte told him. "One hundred eighty-six thousand miles per second, if I'm not mistaken."

"Correct. One hundred eighty-six thousand miles per second. I can travel just a tad under that fast on a good day," Mr. Rodriguez told everyone.

They could only stare in response at this astonishing information.

"Wait, wait, wait," Jericho halted Mr. Rodriguez. "So are you running this fast or flying or," he paused, "how exactly are you getting from point 'A' to point 'B'?"

"Not running or flying, although that would be incredible. I allow Light to envelope my body and then I pretty much just tell it where to go," Mr. Rodriguez explained.

"So you can, in a sense, teleport," Cindy deduced.

"Yupper-dee-doo," he confirmed.

"You're so old dad," JJ said, causing everyone to break into laughter.

"I guess you're right."

"So, wait. Are you saying that we all can teleport?" Jericho asked.

Yes, but no," was Mr. Rodriguez's response.

"Care to elaborate?"

"I didn't just up and teleport one day. I had to first find a way to travel using the light. I made discs of light and rode them, similar to Cindy's rock hoverboard."

"Wow! So it's okay to ride light discs but not rock-boards?" Cindy asked under her breath in a hurt tone.
"No. Both are dangerous. I fell off of one from thirty feet onto my arm. It broke. And four ribs cracked. And two fingers were fractured."
"Oh," Cindy said with obvious regret.

"See? Dangerous," he repeated.

"I can fly," Jericho said.

Right. So you're one step ahead," Mr. Rodriguez told him.

"So what about me and JJ?" Charlotte asked.

"Well, that's something you should ask your father about Charlotte. He might be able to help you learn the skills to develop advanced travel, but, I'll still do my best to help. As for Justin, you may have to develop the skills almost on your own but I will help you in any way I can. Also I believe that Mr. Scott will have to develop his skills almost completely on his own as well, unless he reaches out and says otherwise."

"So when are we gonna practice advanced travel?" Cindy asked.

"First you have to get a handle on your powers. You've summoned the Elementals after you got the Symbols but that's when it's the easiest it'll ever be. You didn't really have to do anything at all, their energy was coursing through you at an exponential velocity. It will be increasingly difficult to summon the Elemental's energy for the first time on your own. We'll start basic Elemental training in the morning. Now, let's try to get some sleep," Mr. Rodriguez told them.

8:45 PM

The Dorms

The group climbed a flight of stairs and arrived in a large open hallway lined with angel white doors. All of the doors were blank except for one at the end of the hall that was inscribed with the Core Symbol for Light.

"So obviously that door is mine," Mr. Rodriguez pointed out.

He walked over to his door and showed them the small metal mechanism beside it.

"This is how my symbol got onto the door. It's called the Scanning Lock Interface Mechanism or the SLIM lock," Mr. Rodriguez told them.

"Why does *literally* everything have an acronym dad?" JJ asked.

"Bro, I was thinking it but you're bold for calling him out on it," Jericho told JJ.

"When we first built CETOBA, we thought it would be cool if everything had acronyms, okay," his dad answered sourly.

"Seems kind of tedious coming up with fitting acronyms. And it also seems unnecessary like why even-," JJ rambled.

"-Dude," Charlotte cut in. "You're being a jerk. Shut up," she demanded. "Continue explaining the SLIM lock to us," she pleaded.

"Alright," Mr. Rodriguez started, "as high tech as this facility is, there are still some procedures that are fairly simple. AVA needs every Elementalist's Core Identity on file and, until recently, it wasn't definitive but now that you have your symbols you can get a Core Identity Scan. As you can see there's four buttons; Lock, unlock, buzz, and scan. To Core Identity Scan you press the 'Scan' button, wait for the scanner on the bottom of the SLIM lock to scan your symbol and then you're set. Only you will be able to unlock your door, anybody else will have to buzz in. When you press unlock your symbol gets scanned each time, so nobody can just barge in your room. The only exception to this is if you use your emergency unlock voice code. To activate entry that way you have to press the scan and unlock at the same time, then say the phrase you selected. The doors will always lock automatically as soon as they close but you can still lock the door from the outside with the lock button. My door is always open and the code is 'Entrez-vous'. Just knock before you enter please," Mr. Rodriguez finished.

"So should we scan our symbols now?" Charlotte asked.

"Yeah you should, if you want to go into your rooms and get some shut eye," Mr. Rodriguez told her.

"Alright then. I'll go first," Charlotte said back. "So I just press scan," she narrated as she pressed the 'Scan' button.

The words 'Please Wait' appeared in white letters on the SLIM screen at the top of the lock and Charlotte rolled up her sleeve, exposing her symbol. The screen counted down from three and Charlotte positioned her arm in front of the scanner. The others watched the purple scanning laser move up and down over the symbol before a single word appeared on the screen.

"Aquarius," Charlotte read aloud and the symbol for water quickly engraved itself into the door. "Well, that was easy."

How does the Symbol get engraved onto the door?" Jericho asked. "I mean, I know we've been walking the line about what is and isn't possible, but that can't be possible right?

A great question indeed. The doors are made of what I call geomorphic alloy, it is composed of the rocks in which the Cores were held. They react with the Elemental energy and can be influenced by the Cores, resulting in a variety of things such as door carving."

"You got an answer for everything, don't ya?"

"Been an Elementalist for a long time. You pick up a few things over the years."

After their brief lesson on geomorphic alloy, the other three simultaneously scanned their symbols and watched them get drawn into the doors.

"Goodnight everyone. Mess hall, no later than nine understand?" Mr. Rodriguez asked.

"Yep," Jericho said.

"Yes sir," Cindy said and saluted him.

"Got it," JJ confirmed.

"Uh huh," Charlotte called out from inside her room.

They all entered their rooms and lay down, resting and preparing for the day ahead of them.

11

THIS IS YOUR PURPOSE
◇ This Is My Creature ◇

MIDNIGHT

TWO DAYS LATER

"Wake up," an unknown voice whispered to Arthur. "Wake up," the voice pleaded. "Wake up, wake up, wake up," it persisted.

Moments of silence passed through Arthur's unconscious mind.

"**ARISE**," the voice demanded.

Arthur snapped awake and was immediately bombarded by the voice's demands.

GET UP! LET'S GO! THERE'S WORK TO BE DONE! CONQUERING! DESTRUCTION! The voice demanded in Arthur's mind.

Arthur was flooded with a searing pain in his head with every single word the voice spoke.

"STOP!" Arthur cried out in pain.

Now why, would I EVER, do a thing like that? The voice asked rhetorically.

"The pain! I can't take the pain!" Arthur yelled aloud at the voice in his mind.

Embrace it. Let it be the coal that fuels the never ending inferno of darkness within you, the voice encouraged.

In response, Arthur screamed in agony.

Now, now. Cowering in the presence of power is just childish, Arthur.

Arthur winced when the voice said his name.

"Wait. You know my name? Who are you?"

My name is my own, Arthur. I was birthed into your mind shortly after you unlocked the place of my imprisonment. Now I am a part of you.

"The Core!" Arthur shouted and began searching through the darkness.

A minute passed and he found nothing in the area surrounding him.

Stop searching, the voice suggested.

"Quiet," Arthur snapped.

Never, the voice said quietly before silencing itself.

"It's gone," Arthur proclaimed after another couple of minutes had passed.

Perhaps, but maybe the abilities have not, the voice chimed.

"The destructive abilities?"

Yes.

"They only work with the Core."

Who can say for sure?

'Well, I don't think you can. I-I've never seen anyone do it."

Exactly. You have only seen that wretched Anthony use the abilities of Light. But, did he have his Core?

"No he, he lost it in the cave."

My point. He did it without a Core. Is Anthony better than you?

"Not a chance in Hell."

Prove it.

"I don't know how."

The voice went silent.

"Oh so now you shut up?"

I was thinking you impatient..., the voice trailed off briefly before speaking again. ***I know what to do.***

Arthur seriously doubted that. "Am I just supposed to believe you?"

The voices laugh bellowed inside of Arthur's mind, filling his head with the intense pain he'd been getting used to.

"Well?" Arthur challenged the voice.

Arthur. You do not know me so-, the voice began.

"-So why the hell would I trust you?" Arthur interrupted.

Shut up! The voice barked. ***I do NOT care what you believe and I do NOT care who or what you decide to put your***

trust in. That is not my purpose. Until you stop living in the memory of what you saw Anthony do all those years ago and grow a pair, you will be this weak shell of what you are to become. You are meant to be the embodiment of Chaos, meaning you have a duty to accept the darkness. Embrace the undying hatred that you've been harboring and command the spread of mayhem, the voice preached. ***"This is YOUR purpose."***

The speech made Arthur's intestines writhe around in his stomach. He took a deep breath and the ground began to rumble. He exhaled, releasing an explosive guttural roar that created a crater around him.

Told you I knew what to do, the voice teased.

"So what are you, like, my better judgment?"

Something like that. I believe I have something that belongs to you.

"Wait I was jok-," Arthur stopped talking and shrieked in pain.

The skin on his arm began to burn away and was replaced with an inky black material. Once the burning stopped Arthur saw the insignia left behind.

Summon the shadows, his better judgment told him.

"What?"

When you bonded with the Core, you called upon the shadows.

"Not intentionally."

You are weak, the voice told him, ***But this is only the beginning. You can not whine like a wounded animal when you do not understand what needs to be done. You must do it. No second guessing. No feeling. Just doing. Do you understand?*** The voice asked, clearly annoyed.

"I do," Arthur confirmed.

His eyes became shrouded in black haze as he concentrated on the shadows around him. He felt himself become a vacuum, drawing in the shadows that surrounded him. As the shadows drew near they collided and melded together taking shape right in front of Arthur's eyes.

"What's going on?" Arthur asked the voice.

"The shadows are forming some kind of creature," the voice spoke eerily through Arthur's lips.

"What the f-," Arthur blurted.

"-Focus! Just focus," the voice interrupted, stealing control of his lips.

The creature the shadows were taking the shape of, was unlike anything Arthur had ever seen. It had six sturdy legs holding up a long slender body. A rounded head with three gnarled horns jutting from it sat firmly upon the long thick neck of the enormous creature. It opened its mouth wide, revealing rows of teeth that were tinted and off-colored, almost purple compared to the rest of his deep dark gray body. When the shadows finished collecting and forming, Arthur was face to face with an eight-foot beast made of pure black shadow. The monster's eyes radiated a deep purple glow. It made no moves towards Arthur, it only stared. Arthur stared back.

"What do I do now, my so-called *better judgment?*" Arthur questioned the voice in his mind.

"That is your creature," the voice told him aloud.

"How do you figure that?"

"You made it, did you not? That was you summoning the shadows, correct?"

"I refuse to answer your obviously rhetorical questions, but I guess you're right," he agreed hesitantly. "This is my creature."

Arthur stared the beast directly in its purple eyes.

"Shadow beast," Arthur said loudly.

My Master, the deep voice of the shadow beast said in Arthur's mind.

"Whoa! Wasn't expecting you to talk back. I have an argument to go finish and I think I'll need a lift. Once I get this out of the way I'll find the other Cores and command all of the powers," he told the beast.

As you wish, the shadow beast said before bowing close to the ground.

Arthur climbed on the creature's back and it hoisted itself back up.

Where to? The beast asked.

"Anthony's house. I have an old friend to visit," Arthur instructed.

That is where Light will fall and Chaos will rise, the voice whispered in Arthur's mind.

"Beast, we have work to do!" Arthur yelled and pointed east.

Yes Master, the shadow beast agreed and took off into the distance.

12

BAH. BOOSH.

◇ Training Day ◇ Part II ◇ Developing Talent

◇

9:17 AM

Mess Hall

JJ walked up nervously to the doors of the cafeteria and checked his phone for the time. 9:17 AM. *Great.* To clear away any suspicion of whether or not he was in trouble, a text from Jericho popped up on the screen.

Bro... Pops is pissed at you...
Wake up and get your ass to the
mess hall ASAP!!!

JJ did what had to be done and pushed the doors open. He immediately jumped into a lecture about punctuality, the very same one he'd heard from his dad a million times. *Blah, blah.* No one respects tardiness. *Blah, blah.* A man's only as good as his word. *Blah, blah.* Early is on time and on time is late. *Blah, blah, blah.*

193

"I don't know why I waste my breath on you. You're first today," Mr. Rodriguez said to JJ, clearly frustrated.

"I went first yesterday," JJ said back defensively as his dad walked away.

His father snapped his head around and shot him an incredibly confused look.

"Did I ask?"

"No but-."

"-But nothing," he snapped. "Eat your breakfast. We are having Elemental Training at ten, AT TEN, and you will be there."

JJ started to speak but Charlotte jumped up from her seat and cupped her hand over his mouth. Mr. Rodriguez told them that he had to get everything ready and left the room. JJ sat down at the table and put his head down. Jericho poked JJ's head with a Cocoa Puffs box.

"So how'd you sleep bro?" Jericho asked JJ, who picked his head up and snatched the box away.

"Great if you must know," he replied sarcastically through a mouthful of dried cereal.

"What time did you wake up?" Charlotte asked.

"The clock was on nine-oh-nine when I looked but I'd been up for a few minutes, so like nine-oh-six, nine-oh-sevenish," JJ answered.

The girls both handed Jericho a five dollar bill and he fanned himself with it, his expression looking as if he'd won a hundred dollars instead of ten.

"You guys bet on me?" JJ asked, mocking the expression of being hurt.

"Told em' you'd be up before quarter past nine and they foolishly disagreed," Jericho explained.

"Never go against a robot," Cindy said.

Everyone laughed. The other three had bowls full of cereal and milk but JJ was content eating the Cocoa Puffs right from the box. They chatted about what they thought would happen during practice.

"I think Uncle Ant is gonna hand JJ his ass on a silver platter again," Cindy told everybody.

"Maybe he'll hit you in the shoulder!" JJ snapped back.
"Not cool," Charlotte said abrasively.

Cindy rubbed his shoulder as silence descended upon the group. Minutes passed and nobody said a word.

"So unrelated," Jericho said, "Air has been abnormally quiet. Granted I've only known It for less than a day but Air seems fairly talkative."

"Now that I think about it," Cindy thought aloud, "after I finished talking with Earth last night I haven't heard from It since."

"Me either," Charlotte said, "but about Water obviously."

They all looked towards JJ for his input on the topic. He looked up and saw them staring.

"Oh, nah, I haven't heard from the cocky bastard who almost killed me yesterday," JJ told them.

Watch yourself kid, Fire warned.

"Never mind," JJ said, "he felt provoked and threatened me. Ooh, scary inside voice," JJ mocked. "Please."

"Can I-uh, talk to It?" Jericho asked nervously.

JJ slammed his Cocoa Puffs on the table and sighed heavily. His eyes began to glow and the next voice from his mouth was Fire's.

"What's up kid?" Fire asked Jericho.

"Why are Air, Water, and Earth not speaking to us?" Jericho asked.

"It's probably because they're in an Elemental meditation stasis," Fire replied.

"Really?"

"No," Fire said blandly. "I have no idea dude, they're your Elementals. All Elementals don't know what the others are doing at all times. That's sorta racist."

"Pause. Rewind. You guys don't have races. You're Elemental space giants trapped inside of rocks, so I think it's a fair assumption that you'd have some sort of connection outside of the Elementalists. I may be ignorant, but I'm not racist. Don't come at me like that," Jericho warned.

"Ooh, the nerdy Elementalist is sooo intimidating. Natasha struck way more fear in me kid, you got big shoes to fill. I mean that figuratively, even though Natasha always wore those giant spiked combat boots."

JJ resumed control of his mouth and his eyes returned to their normal colors.

"That was uncalled for and escalated way out of control," JJ said softly.

Jericho looked at his watch. 9:42.

"I agree. Does anyone know how to get to the Elemental Training Area from here?" He asked.

"No, but lemme try this," Cindy said through a face full of excitement.

"AVA," she called.

There was a moment of silence before the building's AI answered her.

"Yes Cynthia?," AVA responded.

"Ugh. It's Cindy okay."

"Okay Cindy, what can I help you with?"

"How do we get from the Elemental Training Area from here?"

A holographic blueprint of CETOBA's first floor plan with a white line tracing the route from the Mess Hall to the Elemental Training Area materialized in front of everyone.

"Thank you AVA," Cindy said, pleased with herself.
"Will you manage getting there on your own or should I send ADA to assist you?" AVA asked.

"ADA? Who's ADA?" JJ asked.

"ADA - Assisting Directive Android," AVA replied.

"Can we have a moment AVA?" Jericho asked.
"Of course. Call me if you need my assistance," AVA said and went completely silent.

"We can clearly manage on our own," Jericho told everyone, "but I really want to see the android."

"Later, nerd. We have thirteen minutes to get there and we really don't need to be distracted along the way. You'll spend half an hour trying to figure out what makes it tick, and we seriously don't have the time," JJ explained to his friend.

"Come on I wouldn't do that," Jericho insisted.

The others stared at him with skeptical expressions.

"Yeah, you're right, I would. Let's go."

As they prepared to leave Cindy reached out for the map.

"So is this just a hologram or can I," she paused and grabbed at the blueprint, "oh I can." She grabbed the map and said, "It's a physical hologram. Does that even make sense?"

"Honestly, not really," JJ told her. "But I'm sure if we took the time we could definitely figure it out but we only have," he stopped talking and yanked Jericho's arm to check the time on his watch, "ten minutes. We can just ask my dad when we get there."

"Fair 'nuff," Cindy concluded and led the way.

"You're gonna stop manhandling me," Jericho declared to JJ.

"Fight me," JJ taunted with a smile.

"Nah I'm good," he decided after thinking it over for a few seconds.

---

10 AM SHARP
Elemental Training Area

"Who wants to see Justin get put on his ass for being late this morning?" Cindy asked as they walked in.
"I do, I do," Charlotte and Jericho said, mimicking children's voices.

"Good morning to everyone," Mr. Rodriguez called from the practice area. "Today we'll hit a few key points; re-establishing the connection, elemental energy flow, and elemental manipulation. Son, come on over here."

JJ walked over to his dad.

"What do you need me to do?" JJ asked.

"First task is the simplest. Summon the Fire Elemental," his dad instructed.

JJ closed his eyes tightly and concentrated.

Fire, he called.
Yes? Fire responded
You almost murdered me yesterday.
Correct.
Have anything you wanna say about it?
My bad, I guess.
You. Suck.
That's a matter of opinion.
We literally are the only two who can hear these opinions. We're in my, ours? No, my mind right now.
Whatever. Still your opinion.
You know you were a dick to Jericho earlier, right?
That nerd tried to boss up on me, Fire said defensively.
So how does Jericho, his name is Jericho by the way so stop calling him 'that nerd', sticking up for-
-You call him a nerd.
He's my best friend though.
Well, Air is my best friend.
If I ask Air will It agree?
Absolutely. You're not gonna ask though, right?
No, I'm totally gonna ask.
Well then un-absolutely. Air can't stand me.

Wow. I pegged you for the cocky type but that must've taken some rea-

-Even though I'm amazing, Fire interrupted again.

Ugh, JJ thought in disgust. *Wait, what was I talking about?*

How the Air Elementalist, Jericho, is a nerd.

No, but yeah. He was sticking up for himself and you started talking all that noise about his mom.

Well she was highly intimidating and he's not.

Dude, don't talk about his mom.

Fine I won't.

I'm serious.

Me too.

And don't call him a nerd.

Okay.

OKAY?

OKAY!

Cool, now talk to my dad. Please.

Great, Fire said sarcastically. *Big man Light and his bothersome Elementalist, Anthony.*

JJ's eyes glowed red and his dad looked pleased.

"Hello Anthony. Light."

"Hello Fire," Anthony greeted. "Very well done Justin."

JJ's eyes stopped glowing and he was heaving from exhaustion. When he finally managed to somewhat catch his breath, he spoke shakily.

"That's getting more and more tiring to do," he said.

"You have to strengthen the connection between you and your Elemental by practicing Elemental manipulation," Mr. Rodriguez explained. "That's exactly why we're here. To practice."

"So who's next?" JJ asked between breaths.

Charlotte sighed, rolled her eyes and huffed, "Fine. I'm down."

She walked over to JJ and his dad and explained Water's silence.

"Take a second and focus," Mr. Rodriguez told her. "Reach out to Water in your mind and Its energy will come back."

"Okay," she said while closing her eyes tightly.

She extended a mental tether, searching in her mind for her lost Elemental.

Water, she called into the depths of her mind.

Her call seemed to echo throughout her consciousness and moments passed before it was met with a response.

Hello child, water said, her voice like a dream, calming and serene, *what can I do for you?*

I was scared. I thought you'd left me, Charlotte confessed.

I won't leave you until our bond has ended, Water explained.

How will I know?

When the time comes you'll know.

Water?

Yes?

Are you a boy or a girl?

I don't have a human gender, Water answered, *but I could answer to whichever you prefer.*

Charlotte needed less than a second to decide.

I would prefer it if I could refer to you as a female. Please.

Understood.

Can you please talk to JJ's dad?

Of course.

Charlotte's eyes illuminated and Water's soothing voice spoke.

"Anthony," she spoke his name smoothly, "how're you feeling? Light."

"I'm well, Water. How about yourself."

"Fine, thank you. I'll be on my way," she said rather abruptly and Charlotte's eyes clouded before returning to their normal golden brown.

"Jericho, Cindy c'mon. We haven't got all day," Mr. Rodriguez called them over.
"Ladies first," Jericho said to Cindy.

"Okay, I'll wait." She responded with a huge grin on her face and a mischievous glint in her eyes.

Jericho didn't smile back. He stood there with an embarrassed yet serious look on his face and a red tinge creeping up his neck.

"Go!" He demanded.

"You go!" She shot back.

"No, you!" He yelled.

"Ladies first remember?" She screamed.
"Jericho!" Mr. Rodriguez shouted. "you got burned, you go."

"Bah-Boosh!" Cindy gloated, pretending to drop a microphone.

"Can it," Mr. Rodriguez warned.

"Yes sir," Cindy said as she threw up a fake army salute.

Jericho closed his eyes and tried to contact Air.

Hey. Is anybody in here? He asked.

Nope, came Air's sarcastic reply.

Why you gotta be such an a-.

-What do you need? Air interrupted.

Need you to talk to unc for me.

Pass.

You can't pass.

Aw. You're right.

Thank you.

Hard pass.

Motherf-.

-Fine, Air interrupted again.

I. Appreciate. It. Jericho said through telepathically clenched teeth.

Doesn't sound like you do.

What do you want me to do? Beg? Grovel? Plea?

Yes. Any or all of those will do.

Pass.

You can't pass on m-.

Pass.

Stop that you little-.

Pass!

-hole. Ugh, I'll talk to him.

Thank you.

You're a freaking brat.

Shut up, you love me.

Jericho's eyes lit up and Air spoke.

"What Anthony?" Air snapped. "Light."

"Why so crabby?" Anthony mocked.

"I hate this. Bye."

Jericho regained control and looked disappointed.

"That was so bogus," Jericho said. "Air is such a di-," Jericho started but noticed everyone staring including Mr. Rodriguez and quickly decided to change his sentence. "-i-i-isney character," he said quickly.

Nobody seemed impressed by the changed sentence.

"A Disney character?" JJ asked disappointedly. "Do better Jay, do better."

"Anyway. My turn," Cindy announced.

Cindy started to concentrate but, unlike the others, her Elemental spoke first.

Hello there, Earth said. **How are you?**

Good, Cindy replied hesitantly. **How did you-.**

-Know you were calling out to me? I've been ignoring you all morning. I wanted to see how you'd react in my absence. Better than Sylvia if I'm being truthful, Earth told her.

You did that on purpose?

Yep.

And you did it to mom?

Yep. She thought she imagined the whole thing.

You're kinda rude.

You're kinda needy.

Fair 'nuff.

We square?

I think so.

Cool, so I'll talk to Anthony now if you want.

Thanks.

Cindy's eyes glowed and Earth spoke to Anthony.

"Hey ugly," Earth teased. "Light."

"Hey boulder brain," Mr. Rodriguez teased back.

"Brilliant idea, you should make her go first."

"Not a bad idea at all. Thanks Earth."

"My pleasure."

While her eyes still glowed Cindy sarcastically added, "Yeah, thanks Earth."

"Sure thing, my Elementalist," Earth said, and Cindy's eyes stopped glowing.

"Thank you for offering to go first Cynthia," Mr. Rodriguez said excitedly.
"I didn't really off-," Cindy started.

"-Don't care. You'll quickly learn that you and your Elemental are one in the same, so as far as I'm concerned, since Earth offered, you offered," he finished. "We'll start simple," he explained as his eyes began to glow their signature yellow, "just conjure some Earth. Very simple."

"How do I do that?" Cindy asked.

"You should ask your Elemental."

Earth, Cindy said into her mind.

Cinthya, Earth responded.

Cindy, Cindy corrected.

Cinthya, Earth repeated.

We have to make some earth.

Not we, you.

I thought this was a team effort.

The coach doesn't play.

What do you mean by that? You won't help me?

I've granted you complete use of my Elemental Life Force Energy. Take my word, I can do many things but I am now limited by the need to take a host, which is why you have to wield my energy. I will guide you but I assure you that you are in control of all that happens.

Cindy took a deep breath, opened her eyes, which were now glowing deeply, and said aloud, "I understand. It's now or never."

"You've got this," Earth's voice said through Cindy's mouth.

Cindy held her hands out in front of her facing each other and began. Pins and needles instantly prickled every inch of her body. Her heart began to race and she started to scream uncontrollably. The tan aura from around her hands moved erratically and her screaming intensified.

MORE POWER! She managed to scream into her mind.

As you wish, Earth said.

The energy stretched from her fingers and melded together in between her hands. Cindy stopped screaming and concentrated on the mass of energy forming in front of her. A smile crept across her face and there was a loud audible CRUNCH! The energy fell to the floor as a large reddish orange chunk of clay, slightly bigger than a football. The aura faded. Cindy's eyes normalized.

"Bah. Boosh," she said through her beaming smile.

Mr. Rodriguez gave her a drawn out slow clap.

"Most impressive Cinthya. That's exactly what you were supposed to do and what all of the others should hope to do. Good work," Mr. Rodriguez complimented. "You can choose who gets to go next Cinthya."

"Hmm," Cindy chided as she stroked an imaginary beard. "I pick," she paused dramatically, "Char-JJ. Definitely JJ."

"Hey Cindy," JJ called to her.

"What's up?"
"I hate you."

"Aw. Thank you," she said with mock sincerity.

JJ shuffled forward.

"What do I do?" He asked his dad.

"Concentrate, which I know is hard for you-," he told him.

"-BURN!" Jericho yelled.

"Chill out," JJ warned him.

"-and conjure fire," Mr. Rodriguez finished. "Also if you don't mind I'm going to stand behind you."

"Why?" Charlotte asked.

"JJ and fire. Remember October 2012?" Cindy asked, her voice wary.
"Yep, I'm sold," Charlotte said and stood next to Mr. Rodriguez.

The others followed her lead and JJ closed his eyes to concentrate.

Yo! He shouted into his head.
Yes, oh needy one, Fire responded mockingly.
How do I make fire?
Matches, Fire told JJ before bursting into laughter.
Not gonna lie.
What's up?
Kinda hate you right now.

I can't imagine why. I'm delightful.

You're a pain in the ass.

This is true.

Back to the task at hand, how do I conjure fire, Fire.

Think hot thoughts.

What?

Listen kid, you have the ability to do it as long as you feel like you can do it. This ain't about strength or smarts, the Elementalist has to use strong emotional charges as triggers to the Elemental's Life Force Energy aka your powers. So concentrate, think hot thoughts, and look inside yourself to find what fuels your fire.

Woah.

Shit was deep right?

You ruined it.

Shut up, you adore me.

Well...

Get to it fireboy.

JJ opened his eyes and eagerly inspected his limbs, seeing the deep red aura surrounding his body. He turned towards everybody and gave them a hard grin.

"What ya smilin' about dumb-dumb?" Cindy asked in a childish mocking voice.

"This aura sh-," JJ started before remembering where he was and who he was around, "-tuff is wicked."

"Good save," she told him.

"Focus Justin," Mr. Rodriguez sternly reminded him.

"Right, focus," JJ whispered to himself.

> *What fuels my fire? Hot thoughts. Emotional triggers.*
> *Yep,* Fire confirmed.
> *Not now. Trying to concentrate,* JJ snapped.
> *My apologies.*

JJ stuck his right arm out in front of him with the palm turned toward the ceiling and grabbed it firmly with his left. He thought about everything that had happened over the past few days.

> *He and his best friends went on a field trip and found some brightly colored rocks. From space. Aaaand they turned out to not be just rocks but cages, no, Cores, that held space titans made of elemental energy. Aaaand in order for them to live they need to bond with humans, turning them skitzo. Aaaand all of that just-so-happened to happen to him and his friends.*

They were freaking superheroes. All of them.

> *What fuels my fire?* JJ asked Fire.
> *That's the question, isn't it?* Fire asked back.
> *My friends.*

The aura surrounding JJ's outstretched hand began to take shape. It danced around the palm of his hand and played around his fingers. Then, all of a sudden, FWOOSH! A dazzling orange and white fire wrapped itself around JJ's wrist. He was amazed because the heat that he could clearly feel wasn't burning him.

"Ho-ly shit," he said, quickly followed by, "sorry dad. You guys aren't gonna believe this."

"What?" His friends all asked in excited unison.

"I'm fireproof," he told them.

JJ heard Cindy behind him whisper, "*is he serious*," and then Jericho said one word that shattered his friend's whole fireproof bubble.

"Duh."

"Duh?! What do you mean duh?" JJ asked in an incredibly defensive tone.

"You have the Fire Elemental so if you weren't fireproof, that'd be freaking ridiculous bro."

JJ's fire immediately burned away and his face was dismal. He quickly rebuilt his calm façade and asked if he got to pick who goes next.

"Indeed," his father confirmed.

"Bring yourself on up here Gray," JJ instructed like a game show host.

"I'm going to kick your ass if you don't stop calling me Gray," Jericho playfully warned JJ as he walked past him. "Conjure some air, right?" He asked JJ's dad.

"That's right," Mr. Rodriguez told him.

"Shouldn't be too hard," he said confidently.

Air, you there? Jericho asked in his mind.

I'm always here Jericho, I literally can't go anywhere, Air replied in an annoying big brother kind of way.

So, I'm kind of nervous.

Why?

Last time I used my powers I ended up on the brink of death, if you can recall.

Oh right, right. That's valid, but this time won't be like that.

How do you know?

Cause I got you.

Alright, he took a deep breath. *Let's do it.*

Jericho looked at everybody with his glowing white eyes as his aura swayed and said, "This is gonna blow you away."

"Oh for the love of God, jus-just do it already," JJ pleaded. "You're killing me with the puns."

Jericho took a deep breath and his aura started to fade. As he exhaled slowly, his aura returned. He took another deep breath and again the aura weakened. He held this one longer.

Seventeen, eighteen, nineteen, twenty, he counted in his head.

Jericho, you should try exhaling, Air offered.

Twenty-three, maybe, twenty-four, I want, twenty-five, to see, twenty-six, how long, twenty-seven, I can, twenty-eight, hold my, twenty-nine, he continued before Air interjected.

BREATHE! Air commanded.

Jericho uncontrollably forced out all of the air in his lungs and his aura swelled and swirled around him. Within moments, Jericho was hovering a few feet above the floor in a swirling current of air. He maneuvered himself to face the others.

"Hey Pops," he called.

"Yes?" Mr. Rodriguez inquired.

"This is way more difficult than I remember."

"It takes practice."

"Gotcha, gotcha," he confirmed. "Can you take a couple steps to the left? Char and Cindy take a couple to the right."

They all hesitantly complied and left JJ standing alone in place. He locked eyes with his best friend and steeled his expression.

"Call me Gray, one more time," Jericho dared.

JJ's eyes lit up and his hands ignited.

This is gonna be fun, Fire said with unconcealable giddiness.

Oh yeah, JJ agreed, matching his enthusiasm.

"Come at me," JJ said and smiled, before pronouncing the declaration of war slowly. "Gray."

Jericho hurtled himself at JJ. JJ tried to deter him by throwing balls of fire at him but Jericho saw them coming. He thrust his hand out and a whirlwind burst from his palm. It put out the flames just before Jericho's head collided hard into JJ's chest. JJ was quick to recover. He got to his feet and was staring right into his best friend's glowing white eyes. He swung hard but Jericho ducked the punch and hovered backwards. Jericho tried throwing a kick at JJ's side but he caught it and pulled his friend to the ground. JJ stood over Jericho with a flaming fist resting warily above his face. Jericho smiled. JJ smiled back. Their eyes stopped glowing, their auras faded, and JJ helped Jericho to his feet.

"You got a hard ass head, Jay," JJ said, rubbing his chest.

"You got a smart ass mouth, Juss," Jericho fired back.

"Love you bro."

"Love you too bro."

Charlotte broke up their bro-ment.

"Tweedle Dee and Tweedle Dum. In ca-," she started.

"-Am I Tweedle Dee?" JJ interrupted her sentence.

"I didn't really-."

"-No you're Tweedle Dum," Jericho told JJ, cutting into Charlotte's reply.

"Wrong! I'm Dee, you're Dum," JJ clarified.

"False. You're definitely Dum."

"Shut up!" Charlotte screamed. "You're both imbeciles and, in case you haven't noticed, I haven't had a chance to use my powers yet!"

"Oh. Dang. I mean, me and Jericho had our little fight thing," JJ told her.
"I. Know. So shut up before I drown the both of you."

"Let's go Char, show us what you got," Cindy encouraged her as the guys went to stand beside JJ's dad.

Charlotte, Water called to her.

Yeah? She inquired hesitantly.

Concentrate and you should have no problem. We are one in the same, just like Anthony told you. I will allow my strength to flow through your veins just as my power flows through me. Concentrate. Breathe. Feel.

Charlotte kept her eyes closed and concentrated. She took a deep breath and her aura started stretching off of her body and taking shape. It liquified and turned into a crisp, clear water statuette of Charlotte. She opened her eyes, saw the statue, and smiled.

"I was hoping that would happen," Charlotte told everybody.

"That's cool I guess," JJ said under his breath. "Not elemental bro fighting cool or fireproof cool, but still cool."

Charlotte's water statue's head shot off its body and connected hard with JJ's face. His butt hit the floor with a THUD! He got up, wet and flustered, to see Charlotte exploding with laughter.

"You look a little stressed," she teased.

"Next person to knock me to the floor will be eating their teeth," JJ threatened.

His dad snuck up behind him and shoved him to the floor causing the others to burst into raucous laughter.

"You're supposed to make me eat my teeth now," Mr. Rodriguez taunted.

"You got lucky this time," JJ told his father. "Old man."

"I'm sure," Mr. Rodriguez said through laughter. "Now everybody, I want to see glowing eyes. Time to practice. Cinthya, you spar with Charlotte. Jericho, you'll spar with Justin. I'll coach," Mr. Rodriguez finished.

Everybody faced their partner and got into their stances. As their eyes glowed and their auras formed around them, Mr. Rodriguez gave them more instructions.

"I want to see projectile attacks and blocks. One person throws their element, the other blocks with theirs. Then the blocker becomes the attacker, alternating every ten throws. Be careful please, Justin and Cinthya. Try to show a little control. Jericho and Charlotte, you be careful as well for the same yet exact opposite reason."

"Okay," the first two agreed.

"Okay," echoed the second pair.

"Begin!"

13

DO NOT RING THE DOORBELL!

◇ Hunting The Rival ◇

11:34 PM

Outside The Rodriguez Residence

The giant shadow beast thundered down mostly abandoned roads lit by moonlight. Arthur clung inattentively to the beast's back and was talking to the Chaos in his head.

I will kill him, Arthur insisted.

No you will not. You still cling to memories of a brother who long since abandoned you, Chaos reminded him.

You doubt me?

I know you.

You know nothing about me!

I AM YOU! From the moment I chose you and we bonded, we have been bound together as one. I can see all of your memories. I can recite all of the knowledge you have ever obtained. I know your thoughts as they form, your

feelings as they hit you. Every word you have ever spoken. I.
KNOW. YOU.

"Master. We've arrived," the shadow beast informed him.

"Excellent," he responded.

He leapt from the monster's back and walked up to his ex-friend's three story house. He briefly considered pushing the glowing white doorbell but Chaos dismissed the thought.

*You're here to interrogate and **MURDER** him,* Chaos reminded him. ***DO NOT RING THE DOORBELL!***
Arthur agreed and pounded on the door. He waited a few seconds before pounding again. Again he waited. No response. He pounded even harder this time, the door shaking under the weight of his fist.

"I hate waiting," Arthur complained.

As do I, Chaos agreed.

Arthur took a couple steps back from the door, raised his boot, and kicked the door in. Pieces of the demolished door flew into the living room, knocking over picture frames and scattering throughout the room. The house was eerily quiet. He actually kind of liked it. His eyes blackened.

"Shadows," Arthur called out. "Come to me."

Shadows from every object in the room started peeling away from their resting places and surged to Arthur. They gathered at his feet. He raised his hands and they rose from the floor, twisting and convulsing, morphing into four identical beasts. They loosely resembled miniature velociraptors and Arthur was pleased with himself.

"Search the house," he commanded, "and bring me anybody that's here. Alive. Also, any computers and hardware. I'll be here," Arthur finished and sat down in a lounge chair.

"Yes Master," they spoke in guttural unison before rushing off into the depths of the house.

What is the plan? Chaos asked.

"I thought you could hear my thoughts as they form," Arthur said sarcastically.

I want you to vocalize your plan so you do not fuck it up, Chaos snapped.

"Interrogate the people, kill the people, steal the hardware, destroy the house."

Excellent.

"I'm gonna take a nap while they search."

You will do no such thing. Stay alert and await their return.

"Yes sir," he said sarcastically and saluted.

KILL THE SARCASM! Chaos yelled.

"Ugh, kill me now you bossy son of AAUGH!" Arthur screamed. "STOP! STOP! AAAAUGH! PLEASE! PLEASE I'M SORRY!"

YOU. ARE. WEAK. The pain will make you strong. Hopefully it will also eliminate your sarcastic nature. It SICKENS me.

Chaos' mental torture lasted until the shadow beasts returned minutes later.

"Master, the house is empty," the largest of the beasts reported in a scratchy voice. "We have recovered six computers and this is all of the hardware," it finished and gestured to another beast with an armful of various drives and wires.

"Why didn't you put them in a box or something?" Arthur asked, anger biting at the end of the question.

"Box?" The beasts kept repeating as if the concept were exceptionally baffling.

"Go. Get. A BOX!"

The largest beast scrambled to get out of Arthur's sight and go find a box. It was minutes before it came back with an empty broken cardboard box marked, *'Christmas Ornaments.'*

"Lead them to water," Arthur muttered.

The beast holding the drives dropped them into the box and Arthur snatched it away.

"Get out of my sight," Arthur commanded.

The beasts melted into shadowy puddles and returned to their original resting places. Arthur started towards the door but Chaos stopped him.

Remind me, what was step four again? Chaos asked.

"Destroy the house," Arthur answered.
Destroy the house, Chaos mimicked.

"They'll know I was here so they'll be on edge. It will make this whole cat and mouse game more fun. I'll be ready."

You better be. This prolonging is a foolish tactic.

"Shut up. You don't know everything."

Remember this, Chaos warned and went silent.

Arthur shrugged. He walked out of the door and the giant beast he rode in on was lying down in the yard with its eyes closed.

"Beast," Arthur said.

The beast's eyes snapped open.

"Master?" The beast inquired.

"Time to go," he told the beast as he climbed onto its back.

"The destination?"

"316 North Adams Drive."

"Yes Master," the beast said before leaping out onto the road and taking off.

14

I'M ON THE SIDE OF THE FLY

◇ Morals & Feelings ◇

7:45 AM

316 North Adams Drive

"Master, we've arrived," the shadow beast announced.

Arthur jumped from the beast's back with a thud and a silver laptop popped out of the box hitting ground with an audible crack. He picked it up, flipped the screen open, and cursed up at the sky. Cracks were spider webbed across the whole screen. He threw it in the box and turned back towards his beast.

"Abyss, make yourself smaller," he commanded the beast. "Then follow me quietly."

"I am Abyss?" The beast asked.

"Yes, now don't make me repeat myself."

"Yes Master," Abyss said, shrinking down to the size of a fully grown Great Dane.

You are too sentimental, naming it, Chaos told him.

"I thought I told you to shut up," Arthur spat.

As you wish.

Arthur walked to the back of the small brick building. Wooden boards covered the door but he pushed them aside and walked right in, Abyss following behind in silence. Inside was a single room with a small black desk full of papers sitting under a silver desk lamp. A circular brown area rug littered with dirty green stars covered most of the floor. Arthur sat the box on the desk and threw the carpet aside with his foot, revealing a steel trap door. He pulled it open and climbed down the stairs leading to an underground room filled with the dim light of multiple computer monitors sitting around a large white desk. He sat in the padded chair and scooted close to the monitors. Abyss walked up to his master's side as he typed away on the keyboard.

"Go get the box from upstairs," Arthur ordered.

Without hesitation Abyss vanished in a cloud of darkness while Arthur typed up a password decryption algorithm. When Abyss returned with the box of electronics, Arthur plugged a USB from his computer into a sleek black laptop and ran the algorithm. He attached USB's into the rest of the computers and hardware and put them on standby, so the algorithm would run through them, one after the other.

Now what? Chaos asked impatiently.

"I'm hungry," Arthur admitted.

Of course you are, Chaos said. ***Humans. Always eating.***

"Anyway, there's a cozy little diner a few miles away from here so, I'll go eat and have a little pie before I finally get a chance to quench this bloodlust," he finished and chuckled quietly to himself.

9:15 AM
Jimmy's Diner

Arthur took a big swig of pink lemonade and stared down his last forkful of pie.

"Oh my God, I'm so full," he groaned.
Then stop eating you gluttonous swine, Chaos snapped.

A tall, brown haired, pale-skinned waitress wearing a 'Hi My Name Is... Cauleen' name tag, walked over to Arthur with a little black folder and a smile.

"Hey, hey. Can I get ya anything else dear?" She asked him in a southern accent.

"Uh," Arthur started and surveyed the room.

There were nine customers and three waitresses. Clearly there were some kitchen staff but he'd deal with them later.

"Actually there is," he told her.

She waited patiently for his request.

"Your life."

Her face contorted into a mixture of terror and confusion. She timidly cleared her throat.

"Ex-excuse me?" She stuttered the question.

"Well I wouldn't say you could get it for me," he explained.

He scooped the last forkful of pie into his mouth while fear radiated off of the waitress. His eyes blackened and his eerie black aura seeped from his skin and pulsed around him as he turned back to her and spoke calmly.

"I'm going to take it."

She looked into the depths of his eyes and let loose a spine chilling wail. Arthur smiled. He jumped to his feet and grabbed her by the throat. All eyes were on them now. He threw his hand out to the side. The table's shadow lurched into his palm and morphed into a small blade. He thrust the blade into the bottom of her chin, twisted it abruptly, and watched her mouth fill with blood and her life drain away. He dropped her lifeless body to the tiled floor. Two guys decidedly wanted no part in the same fate and ran for the door.

"Abyss!" Arthur yelled.

Arthur's own shadow left from behind him and swam along the floor towards the door. As the men were steps away from escaping, Abyss rose from the floor blocking the exit. Abyss snarled at them, showing off Its assortment of jagged teeth, and they immediately surrendered, backing away slowly.

"Everybody, we can do this one of two ways," Arthur announced. "You can all come out, stay calm, and accept your fate or you can panic and die anyway." Arthur waited.

Without warning, a wave of panic swamped over the diner.

"Option two then? This'll be fun," he declared with a smile.

Kill them, Chaos agreed.

Arthur hurled the knife at one of the men who'd tried to escape but was now crouched underneath a table dialing someone. It connected with the phone first before stabbing through his hand, pinning it to the wall.

"Abyss. Watch the others 'til it's their turn," Arthur commanded.

Abyss multiplied, becoming three cheetah sized Abysses and they said, "Yes Master," in unison and obeyed the command. Arthur summoned the weapon and it flew out of the wall into his hand. The man was crying out in pain.

"Shh, it's almost over," Arthur said in a pitiful attempt at being soothing as he walked over to his next victim.

The man cried louder, taking no comfort in his attacker's cool headedness. Arthur smacked the side of the table and it flew across the restaurant, smashing into pieces against a wall. He bent down and pressed the blade against his neck, cleanly slitting the man's throat. The man's head slumped into his chest which was now being covered in his own thick red blood. Arthur's skin began to buzz. He'd never enjoyed anything quite this much before. He spotted the next victim, a short teenage blonde girl wearing a sparkly green blouse. He rushed over to her so fast he felt as if he were gliding around the restaurant.

He held her face and stared deep into her dazzling blue eyes. She stared back, captivated by those demonic pitch black eyes that portrayed death and destruction.

"Your eyes are absolutely beautiful," Arthur complimented her, his voice an octave lower than usual.

"Thanks," the girl squeaked.

"What's your name, pretty eyes?"

"Master, these humans are restless," one of the Abysses cut in.

Arthur turned toward the Abyss and screamed, "Corner them and stay silent! If they step out of line, slaughter them or I'll slaughter you!"

He snapped his attention back to the girl.

"Name," he said, his voice menacingly calm.

"N-name?" She asked, confused.

"Yes, yours. What is it?"

"M-M-Monica."
>   ***Stop toying with her and kill her***, Chaos demanded.
>   ***Shut up***, Arthur shot back.

"Darling Monica," he whispered, "keep your eyes on me. You won't feel," he plunged the blade into her heart and twisted, "a thing." Her head lolled into his hand and he dropped her to the floor. "Such a shame," he monologued, "her eyes were truly captivating. *A veces los inocentes deben morir,* I guess."

Arthur addressed the frightened people cowering away from his beasts.

"Now, it's time for you all to die. I'd apologize but I'm not remorseful. Abyss, kill them," he ordered.

Without hesitation the Abysses attacked. One of the three clamped its jaws around a man's torso, his severed legs and upper body fell to the floor in a bloody mess. Another one pinned a cook to the wall and decapitated her with a single swipe of its giant paw, splattering the others with blood.

"FUCK! It's in my mouth! Oh my god, it's in my fucking mouth!" A tall middle-aged man screamed before vomiting in his lap.

Arthur walked over to the man while the Abysses created carnage all around him. He bent down and touched the nauseous man's shadow, which crept up his arm and created a shadowy sleeve.
"Why?" The man asked in a faint Russian accent, tears in his eyes.

"Why what? Be more specific," Arthur demanded menacingly.

"Why are you killing us? What did we do?"

"I'm not accusing anyone here of doing any wrong," Arthur explained.

A long, skinny, brown arm landed beside them. Arthur picked it up and threw it to an Abyss who caught and ate it.

"You see," he turned back to the man, "a man who clings to things like morals and feelings, only kills out of necessity. Do you have morals and feelings mister," he paused.

"Axton. Avi Axton," he told Arthur.

"Arthur Arkaine. Doctor by choice if you can believe it. Anyway do you have morals and feelings Avi?"

"I do."

"So you'd kill a fly if you had a swatter handy, even if the fly were merely buzzing around, doing basic fly things?"

"Of course. It doesn't belong in my space so naturally."

"Abyss," Arthur beckoned his beast.

Abyss had transformed back into one grizzly bear sized being and walked over. Its face and mouth dripped with the blood of the innocent.

"Master?" Abyss asked awaiting its orders, breath smelling of the freshly deceased.

"Avi, I have a secret," Arthur confessed.

"What is it?" Avi asked shakily.

"I don't have morals or feelings."

"I don't understand."

"Well, let me explain."

Arthur leaned in close to Avi's ear.

"Everyone would swat the fly, except me. I'm on the side of the fly, the underdog, the weakling. The fly has no choice but to buzz around and look for food, that's just what flies do and since it can't swat you for simply being a ruthless human, I'll help turn the tables," he said as he touched the shadow covered hand to Avi's forehead.

On the wall behind him, a silhouette of an Avi sized fly appeared.
"You're the fly, Avi," Arthur whispered.

Horror painted a mask over Avi's face as he comprehended the analogy.

"Abyss," Arthur said.

"Master?" Abyss repeated.
"Swat the fly."

10:30 AM

The Underground Lab

"Thirty-four percent," Arthur read the diagnostics aloud. "It will be six hours before it's completely finished."

So? See what it has uncovered so far, Chaos told him.

"Obviously."

Arthur clicked on the storage folder and opened a program that searches for commonly visited files. He set it loose on the files and started skimming through the emails.

"Damn this is a lot."

Better get to work, Chaos told him.

15

THE PROBLEM & THE PLAN

◇ No Ifs. No Ands. No Buts. ◇

10:15 AM
Approaching The Rodriguez Residence

"Oh whoa oh, I would go through all this paaain, take a bullet straight through my braaain, yes I would die for you baby, but you won't do the same," everybody sang along with the music.

Mr. Rodriguez turned the music down, stirring up a bit of confusion.

"-beat me till I'm-hey. What gives?" JJ asked.

"Shh. We're getting a strange vibe the closer we get to the house," he told everybody.

They were right around the corner from the Rodriguez Residence when Mr. Rodriguez pulled the vehicle to the curb. He turned the car off and got out.

"What is he doing?" Charlotte asked JJ.

"How should I know?" He asked back.

"He's your da-," she started before Mr. Rodriguez stuck his head in the window.

"-Something's wrong," he explained, "Light feels it as well. All of you get out and follow me quietly."

The four of them jumped out of the car and crept behind JJ's dad as he slowly approached his house. Mr. Rodriguez peeked around his hedges and saw the front door busted inward.
"Damn," Mr. Rodriguez whispered.

"What?" JJ asked.

"Front door's busted in."

"You think somebody's in there?"

"Only one way to find out," Mr. Rodriguez told him and slowly walked the driveway.

When he was at the doorway he turned around to the others. His eyes started to glow.

"Stay here. We'll be back," Light told them before Mr. Rodriguez took off into the house.

They watched JJ's dad disappear into the house and waited. Countless minutes of silence passed as they stared at the doorway awaiting his return. They caught a brief glimpse of him as he passed the entrance and headed upstairs. Again they waited. He returned and told them the house was clear. Jericho checked his watch.

"Holy crap!" He shouted. "We've been standing in the yard for forty-nine minutes."

"Didn't even feel that long," Charlotte told him.

"That's irrelevant," Mr. Rodriguez told them. "Come inside and call your parents. Tell them it's about the Core Elementals. I have to make a call of my own," he finished and walked inside.

Once everyone was inside they called their parents and Mr. Rodriguez retreated to his study.

"Who do I call?" JJ called after his father.

"I don't care," his dad told him and shut the door.

11:05 AM

Mr. Rodriguez' Study

"Are you sure it's a good time?" The female voice on the other end of Mr. Rodriguez' line asked.

"Pam, we talked about this," he told her. "A day would come when you'd have to bring him back. Not to mention he bonded with a Core and his Symbol will appear today."

"Anthony, he's my baby."

"He's my son!"

The conversation stilled.

"I know," she said. "We'll be there."

"Thank you. I-I uh-," he started but stopped himself.

"I know. See you soon, Sunshine," she said and hung up.

Anthony took his glasses off and set them on the desk. He rubbed his temples and took a deep breath.

He exhaled and whispered to himself, "Today's gonna be a long day."

11:45 AM
Rodriguez Residence

"We all know why we're here," Mr. Rodriguez said to the other nine people who sat around his living room.

Zach and Pamela, Charlotte and her father Oliver, Cindy and her mom Sylvia, Jericho and his guardian Stephanie, and JJ.
"It's about the rocks, right?" Zach asked.

Everyone except Zach, Pamela, Mr. Rodriguez, and Stephanie simultaneously muttered '*Cores,*' so instead of a whisper it was more like a hushed speaking voice.

"Don't worry, I don't feel attacked," Zach announced sarcastically.

"Yes, it's about the Cores Zach. More accurately, the danger the Core Elementalists are in."

"Is that why you're door's broke in?" Oliver asked.

"Yep. There's a new keeper of Chaos," he explained. "He was here, in my home, while I was at CETOBA. He stole my hardware and computers and it appears he's a loose cannon now. Justin, press play."

JJ picked up a remote and played the video that was cued up on the television. It was a woman giving a local news report from a small town in Oregon. The caption read '15 Dead At Jimmy's Diner.'

"Good afternoon. I am Joanna Markell with Channel Nine News and I am currently standing outside of a gruesome scene at the beloved Jimmy's Diner. A local bystander stumbled across the carnage at around noon and alerted the authorities. It seems that an attacker and an animal brutally murdered and mutilated all of the workers and patrons in the establishment. So far six bodies have been identified but they are working on finding out who the other nine people were. Jimmy's is set to close but for how long, who's to say? Police are asking anyone with any information to contact local authorities. We'll have more on this story as it develops. Again, I'm Joanna Markell, Channel Nine News," she finished.

Everyone stayed silent. JJ turned the tv off and placed the remote on the coffee table as quietly as he could.

"Arkaine did that?" Cindy asked quietly.

"Yes," Mr. Rodriguez answered. "He's the Mayhem Core Elementalist and it looks like he's already been corrupted by Chaos. He'll have no problem killing innocents and it seems that he can control the beasts."

"Damn, this is really happening again," Sylvia said. "How much training have they done?"
"Not much," Mr. Rodriguez confessed. "We just started. They have about two days under their belts. It takes time to get a handle, you know that."

"They don't have time Anthony!" Stephanie shouted.

"Even if they rushed, it still takes time, Stephanie. They have to get a handle on tapping into the energy."

"Pops, all I'm saying is they need to hurry and get a handle or everyone in this room is in for more danger than they can handle."

"Look," Oliver said, "they have a month of school left so let's just pull them and then they'll just train until they get it."

"Whoa, whoa, whoa," JJ cut in, "I do not wanna spend the whole summer training."

"We'll need to make a schedule or something because I feel what JJ's saying," Jericho added. "But I also agree we do need to train because Arkaine's gone full effin' psycho."

"Look! We'll iron out the details but as far as I'm concerned, training is top priority," Mr. Rodriguez said.

The other parents agreed.

"Now kids, let me see your eyes," Mr. Rodriguez instructed as his eyes turned yellow.

The four of them followed suit and one after the other, their eyes began to glow and their auras enveloped them.

"I miss that," Oliver and Sylvia said at the same time and laughed.

"Anybody want to-," Mr. Rodriguez started to ask but the question was cut short by Zach screaming in agony.

A glowing orange symbol seared itself into his forearm. He calmed himself as the others watched and when the pain flitted away, he saw the Magma Symbol.

"Don't miss that," Oliver said and rolled up his sleeve, revealing a blue tinted scar identical to Charlotte's Symbol.

"That's awesome daddy," Charlotte told him excitedly.
"Yeah. The after effects usually are," he told her.

"I guess all of us actually have corresponding Symbols and scars," Sylvia said, "except Stephanie. And Anthony. And Zach and Justin and Jericho," she paused. "I didn't think that thought all the way through."

"And mom," Zach said.

"Of course, and Pamela," she added quickly, although Pam stayed quiet and reserved.

"Right mom?" Zach asked somewhat nervously, an unnecessary suspicion brewing.

"Mhmm. Course baby," his mom unconvincingly confirmed.

"Not to be forward but can you please pull up your sleeve?" JJ asked as politely as he could.

"JJ!" Charlotte shouted and decked him in the arm.

"Woman!" He shouted back, rubbing his arm.

"Why're you coming at my mom bro?" Zach asked angrily.

"I'm not," he said defensively.

"Zachary, calm down," his mom demanded.

He took a deep breath and he seemed to settle down. Mr. Rodriguez met Pamela's eye and he nodded at her.

"Pull up your sleeve please Pam," Mr. Rodriguez asked.

She cautiously obliged and rolled up her sleeve. There was nothing to be seen.

"Everybody satisfied?" Mr. Rodriguez asked.

"Yup," JJ answered.

"Good," Stephanie said. "What's the plan? I have work at 12:30."

"They'll finish this upcoming week, then we'll move them to CETOBA where they'll do daily training until they have the skills necessary to protect themselves. After that, well I guess we'll just have to play it by ear. How's that sound?" Mr. Rodriguez finished.

"I mean, do we really have a choice?" Jericho asked. "This seems like something that you all are gonna decide with or without our approval. So you guys tell us, are we doing this shit or not?"

"Jericho!" Stephanie snapped.

"Tell him he's wrong Steph," Cindy cut in.

Stephanie said nothing. The other adults didn't negate the idea either.

"Exactly," Jericho declared.

"Look, throughout the week we can iron out the details but for right now, this is the plan," Mr. Rodriguez announced.

"Fine. I have to get to work," Stephanie said.

"Everyone has to be extra careful now Steph," Jericho told her. "I'll come with you."

"I am a grown woman. I can go to work by myself."

"I know that but-."

"-But nothing Jericho," she said loudly.

"Stephanie! It can't hurt."

An awkward quiet passed through the room as all eyes were rested on Stephanie and Jericho.

"Fine," she conceded. "I'll see you all very soon, I'm sure."

Stephanie got up from her seat, said her goodbyes, thanked JJ's dad for the hospitality, and left with Jericho following behind her.

After they left Mr. Rodriguez got up and paced around the room. He became so lost in thought that the whole world melted away, leaving him and Light alone in his mind.

This is bad, Anthony. Very, very bad, Light warned.

How do we counter? He asked.

When Chaos comes there will be a fight.

There always is.

So prepare them for battle. Arthur hates you. Chaos is undoubtedly stoking that hatred, so anyone you associate with is in danger. He has all of your computers, files, and emails so it's only a matter of time.

Where there's smoke there's fire. I agree that we have to prepare them for the fight. But what if I-.

-You can do this Anthony. Oliver, Sylvia, Natasha, and Pamela all had their time as Elementalists but your time as the Light Bearer is far from over. You are the strongest human being I've ever seen and I have no uncertainty that you will train the next generation of Elementalists to fight Chaos and emerge victorious. You have to have the same amount of faith in yourself as I have in you.

"Anthony! Anthony! ANTHONY!"

Mr. Rodriguez snapped out of his trance and found himself being yelled at by Oliver.

"I'm okay Ollie," he assured him. "Listen up. Chaos is coming. As of right now, we have one week to get our shit in order before we get off the grid. No ifs. No ands. No buts. If you're not in a safe place, you're likely to be killed. He's killing innocents and it's only a matter of time before he has all of my hardware data and a complete hit list with everybody's name on it. I love you all, even you Zach and Pam. You're part of this family now and I protect my family. No. Matter.

What. So go home, pack your stuff. Call your jobs, your families, your friends. Get your shit in order because by Saturday morning we have to be gone. I know it's sudden but what has to happen, has to happen. I'm sorry. Now let's get to it," he finished and left the room.

The room sat uncomfortably with the heavy declaration. No one knew what to say, so no one spoke. They just sat quietly. Oliver tapped Charlotte on her arm. She looked at him, hoping he'd speak and say something worthwhile but all he did was get up and walk toward the door. Charlotte understood and quietly got up to follow him. She dapped up all of her friends and walked out behind her dad. They left and the rest of the guests soon followed after. Two by two the room emptied in silence until JJ sat alone in his living room. He got sick of the silence and retreated to his bedroom and flopped onto his bed.

"Fuuuuuck," he whispered to himself. "They never write about any of this bullshit in the comics. Not once have I read about five families having to jump off the face of the Earth together to avoid being murdered by a psychopathic homicidal maniac."

Every legend's origin story is unique, Fire said quietly.

"Fuck life man," JJ whispered to himself as he rolled over and drifted into a much needed sleep.

16

GETTING SHIT IN ORDER

◇ Well, You Tried ◇

8:00 AM
Lambent Solar Systems Inc.

Mr. Rodriguez stood at the head of a long conference table facing the most powerful of his building's associates. They patiently waited for him to start the meeting. It was time for him to start getting his shit in order.

"Good morning all," he greeted. "Some, complications, have surfaced and for reasons I can't disclose I am forced to terminate this facility's operations until further notice."

This caused a wave of anger, confusion, and panic to surge the room.

"Sir, you can't be serious!" One man shouted.

"We have families to take care of Anthony!" A portly woman shrieked.

"You can't do this!" Another woman cried.

Screams of anger and concern were spit at Mr. Rodriguez from every direction. All of them along the lines of how he was an inconsiderate monster and a selfish egomaniacal tyrant. He broke through their cries of rage.

"LISTEN!" He shouted. "I understand that this news is troubling bu-."

"-Troubling? Troubling! This move is disastrously life-altering!!" A tall black man yelled as he jumped up from his seat.

"Sylvester, hear me out. ALL OF YOU, hear me out! Every person working in this facility will receive a year's salary and a recommendation of relocation statement upon departure. I want to stress that you are not being fired, you can go work in any other LSSI facility in the country but, you simply cannot work in *this* building any longer. For your safety I'm going to need you to trust me. You all will start work in any facility of your choosing in ninety days, so go enjoy a well-earned paid vacation. Are there any final questions or comments?" He asked.

No one spoke up.

"Dismissed," he said, swooping up his briefcase from the floor. He left the conference room and everyone followed him out.

10:00 AM
Third Period Gym

"Look man, all I'm saying is if there's no oxygen, there's no fire, ergo air supersedes fire," Jericho explained to JJ as they jogged around the gym.

Preach, Air chimed.

"Bro you don't control oxygen, you control air," JJ paused to gather his thoughts.

Facts, Fire threw in.

"And yeah, the air consists of oxygen and stuff so I guess there's some validity but you can't take away the air if I burn your ass to a crisp first, you feel me?" He asked right before a heavy arm crashed into his back, knocking him to the floor.

A wide, freckle-faced, red haired moron turned around, pointed at JJ, and laughed loudly. Bradley Reinbeck. He'd been messing with JJ ever since he'd moved to San Diego in the seventh grade. JJ hated his guts and informally declared Bradley as his mortal enemy.

"Watch your step dumbass," Bradley called to JJ, which made Bradley's cronies, Charles and Vince, burst out laughing.

Jericho reached down to help JJ up but when their hands touched, Jericho pulled away.

"Dude, simmer down," Jericho told him.

"What're you talking about?" JJ asked as he boosted himself off of the floor.

"Look. That's what I'm talking about," Jericho said and pointed to the floor where JJ was sitting.

JJ looked down and saw his handprints lightly burned into the hardwood. He looked at Jericho for a few seconds and then he looked back at the floor.

"I see what you're talking about," he told him.

"Yeah no shit."

"I'll fix it."

"How?"

"Justin! Jericho! Quit lollygagging and put some fire under your ass before the whole class runs suicides!" Coach Gibson called to them from across the gym.

"Just a sec coach, I'm lacing up my shoe!" JJ called back as he bent down.

"Alright. Jericho let's go!"

Jericho took off and JJ kept his eyes down as they began to glow and his aura clung tight to his body. He extended his index finger, which glowed white with heat, and traced boxes around the handprints and filled them in. He did his best to crouch over his work in a poor attempt to hide his misdeed.

What do you think? JJ asked his Elemental.

I think they won't trace it back to you directly if they even trace it back at all, but unless you start moving somebody's bound to notice, Fire told him.

JJ agreed, got up, and started jogging around the gym with the rest of the class again. He caught up with Jericho just as the warm-ups ended. They went and sat on the bleachers as Coach Gibson and two other students went to the storage closet and came out with bags full of red rubber balls. They laid them out in the middle of the gym and everyone knew exactly what they were doing.

"Line up!" Coach Gibson yelled and blew his whistle.

Everyone lined up against the wall and waited to be picked by the team captains, Bradley Reinbeck and Beverly Smalls. Jericho and JJ ended up on Beverly's team, mostly because Bradley wanted to throw anything he could at JJ.

The first game went smoothly enough, Jericho was third out on their team and JJ was seventh. When the second game kicked off, things escalated quickly. As soon as the game started, Bradley grabbed a dodgeball and sent it full throttle on a direct path to JJ's face. JJ had no idea what was happening but looked up just in time to see the flying face-smasher barreling towards him.

Shit, he and Fire said at the exact same time, not even a second before the impact.

JJ heard the rubbery sound of connection before he saw nothing. His face was stinging and no matter how hard he tried he couldn't manage to open his eyes through the pain. When he finally got his eyelids under control he saw Coach Gibson kneeling over him and the rest of the class huddled around them. He did a quick search of the students and found the asshole responsible for the unnecessary pain pulsing through his face. Bradley. JJ pushed himself up off of the ground and walked directly up over to Bradley. He put a finger on his chest and lowered his voice.

"You and me, after class. Coach won't care and you're gonna get exactly what you deserve," JJ told him.

Bradley shoved JJ's arm off of his chest.

"Whatever. I ain't scared of you or your little nerdy sidekick. I'll whoop both your asses without breaking a sweat," Bradley said with subtle confidence.
"That's enough," Coach Gibson said. "JJ, you okay?"

"Yeah," he told Coach Gibson.

"Need the nurse?"

"No Coach."

"Then back to dodgeball," he announced.

"You heard what I said," JJ said to Bradley as he walked away.

"Whatever," Bradley said back.

Gym flowed smoothly after the altercation. The class played four more relatively injury free games before the end of class bell rang. Jericho walked over to JJ and they walked to the locker rooms together.

"You good?" Jericho asked.

"Never better," JJ assured.

They were in the locker room for less than ten seconds before JJ was thrown into the thick of it. Bradley pushed him up against the lockers and punched him in the face. His fist connected with JJ's right cheek which rattled him a little, but JJ already figured Bradley would get the first hit. He was prepared for this. JJ pushed Bradley off of him, causing him to topple over the bench and fall on his back. It took no time for JJ to be on top of Bradley, hitting him with right after left after right after left. JJ went to get another lick in but was hit in his side by another attacker. He looked over and saw the tangled mop of dirt brown hair belonging to Bradley's friend Vince, who was readying to punch JJ in the face. *Nope.* JJ dipped left as Vince swung, avoiding the punch but giving Bradley a chance to regain his composure, and he shoved JJ off him and got to his feet.

Bradley and Vince were now standing over JJ, pummeling him, when Jericho ran over and threw a well-executed palm heel strike into the side of Vince's head. Vince went limp and crashed head first into the lockers. Vince's body slumped on the floor and didn't move except for the motions of breathing. Jericho's attack caught Bradley off guard and he went to check on his friend. Jericho helped JJ off of the floor.

"Good job," JJ said to Jericho, "and thanks again."

"Thanks and of course," Jericho said back.

"Let's finish up here."

JJ walked over to Bradley and lifted him to his feet by his shirt before throwing him into the lockers, adrenaline coursing through his veins. Since when was he this strong?

> *Fire,* JJ called.
> *JJ?* Fire inquired.
> *I need you to scare this dude.*
> *How?*
> *Shitless.*

A terrifyingly happy laugh echoed through JJ's mind. *Is there any other way?*

JJ brought his face uncomfortably close to Bradley's and his eyes started glowing while his aura swayed around him. Jericho saw what was happening and herded everyone close enough out of sight of his best friend.

"This'll be the last time," Fire told Bradley. *"Next time, you won't get to open your goddamn eyes again. I will fucking end you, ya feel me?"*

"Uh-huh," Bradley agreed shakily.

"And feel free to tell people about the glowing eyes," Fire told him as JJ let Bradley off of the lockers. *"It won't sound as crazy as the fire,"* he finished, raising an emblazoned hand and putting a fiery finger to his lips.

JJ's eyes stopped glowing, the fire went out, and he just left Bradley standing there, looking like he'd just seen a ghost. He walked around the corner and saw Jericho attempting to hold people back.

"What's up?" Jericho asked.

"Nothing man, just had to get shit in order," JJ told him.

"We good?"

"Always."

2:17 PM
Corridor C

Cindy looked at her best friend who was sweating underneath her messy bangs.

"You okay Char?" Cindy asked.

"Mhmm. Gotta get my shit in order right?" She asked back, clearly nervous.

"You got this," she encouraged.

I agree, Water told Charlotte. *Your dispute seems trivial so ending the affair should be fairly simple.*

Right, Charlotte said to Water, sounding very unconvinced.

"Water thinks so too," Charlotte told Cindy. "Go to class, I'll see you in a bit."

"Okay," she said and gave Charlotte a big hug. "I love you Char."

"I love you too."

Cindy walked off into the opposite direction of the tall mocha-skinned girl staring into her locker. Her hair was brown like cinnamon and her golden brown eyes sparkled like amber. All in all, she was one of the prettiest girls Charlotte had ever seen in her life. She had pretty big boobs and her butt was way bigger than Charlotte's, not to mention she stayed in shape by captaining the swim team. She intimidated the hell out of Charlotte.

"Tonya," Charlotte said a little quieter than she'd meant to.

Tonya's expression dropped into a look of disgust and anger at the sight of Charlotte.

"I'll never understand why he likes you so much," Tonya said to her.

"Look. I've told you before, I do not like JJ like that so y-."

"-But he likes *you,* like that."

"I've made my feelings clear to him. What do you want me to do about it?"

"Nothing," Tonya said and shut her locker loudly.

She tried to walk away but Charlotte grabbed her arm firmly and stopped her. Tonya was surprised at Charlotte's boldness and turned to hear her out. She shrugged her hand off of her arm and stared daggers directly into her soul. Charlotte cleared her throat.

You've got this. I'm right here, Water whispered.

"Whatever, *this*, is between us needs to be handled."

"Why?"

"Because I wanna squash it."

"But why? What does *Charlotte* get from deading the issue?"

"I don't know, peace of mind? Resolution? Closure?"

"No."

That single word caught Charlotte off guard.

"No?" She asked, completely questioning Tonya's motives.

"Yeah. No. I don't owe you any of those things," she callously explained.

"But why can't we j-."

"-Ugly little bitch."

Well, you tried, Water said, already sensing Charlotte's next move.

Charlotte honestly felt like she was just going through the motion, not even in control of her body, but her fist swung quickly and forcefully. It connected with Tonya's mouth and the punch threw her off balance, causing her to stumble backwards a couple of steps. When Tonya looked back up at Charlotte, whose face was now oozing regret, she felt a wetness running down her chin. Her lip had been busted open and she hadn't noticed that her mouth was now pooling blood. She wiped her face and looked down at her hand, causing the saliva-blood mixture to splash into it.

"I am so, so, so, SO sorry," Charlotte frantically apologized.

Tonya raised her bloody hand and slapped Charlotte across her face. Charlotte looked at Tonya and stoned her visage.

"I deserved that," Charlotte told her.

"Fucking right," Tonya agreed. "Now take me to the nurse and we're square."

Charlotte walked Tonya to the nurse's office and explained the situation as best she could. As they got tended to and washed up, Charlotte took her phone and shot a quick text to Cindy.

Me and Tonya are cool. #TotallySquashedIt

Good job my Elementalist. I'm very proud, Water told her.

Thank you Water, Charlotte said back, also proud of what she'd accomplished.

4:45 PM
The Underground Lab

"It's finally finished," Arthur said with a sigh of relief. "There looks to be a lot of mention of something called Kah, no Cee, yeah, CEE-TOH-BAH. CETOBA"

What is that? Chaos asked.

"If I knew then you'd know, wouldn't you?" Arthur asked sarcastically.

I suppose.

"I suppose," Arthur mimicked. "Smart ass idiot."

Arthur skimmed the material as quickly as he could while still retaining the information contained within. He gained knowledge of the other Core keepers or Elementalists, as they called themselves. He learned that there had been multiple Elementalists within the course of the last twenty-five years and probably many that had yet to be found. He finished reading every last piece of information about the Elementalists and CETOBA that he could find and got up from his chair. He grabbed a small dry erase board and marker from the tiny closet behind the monitors and sat back down. He wrote down a few things about CETOBA that he knew for sure.

Things I Definitely Know About CETOBA

1. Secret base where Elemental skills get perfected
2. Super safe and well hidden = virtually undetectable
3. Limited amount of people have knowledge of its whereabouts
4. Anthony built it with help of at least three people;

oliversanti13234@lambentsolarsystems.com

pamelas@yahoo.com

sylviaaivlys@lambentsolarsystems.com.

Arthur went to the website linked to the emails, which he knew was Anthony's company, and ran through the directory trying to identify two of the addresses. After a quick search he came up with the identities Oliver Santiago and three different Sylvias; Sylvia Clark, Sylvia Madison, and Sylvia Thompson. He cross referenced the length of time they'd all worked for the company against how long

Oliver had worked for the company and deduced that the Sylvia he was looking for, was Sylvia Thompson. So he searched them up on Google to find their home addresses and plotted his next course of action.

"I think we go see what this Sylvia Thompson and Oliver Santiago know about CETOBA, the Cores, and the Elementalists," Arthur said aloud to Chaos.

Sounds good. Do not fuck it up*,* Chaos told him.

"You need to fix your attitude 'cause I swear you're a freaking buzzkill."

Shut up and go get your shit together.

"Yes sir, Mr. SuperFuckingBuzzkill. Abyss let's go," Arthur ordered and he and Abyss left the lab, mounted up, and took off.

17

FROM POINT A TO B

◇ Your Silence Is Truly A Blessing ◇

2:00 AM *THE FOLLOWING FRIDAY*
Rodriguez Residence

"You literally have no packing skills whatsoever," Cindy criticized JJ while he tried to stuff a suitcase into the trunk of his dad's Escalade. "It's not going to fit!"

"Forget you," he grunted. "I'm a Tetris legend."

"On what planet? Just put it in Violet and let's go."

"No and that name is stupid because your car is tan."

"Justin! Put it in her car or leave it," his dad demanded out of his driver side window.

JJ complied and walked over to Cindy's car. When she popped the trunk, he shoved his suitcase in and slammed it closed. As he walked back by her to get to his car she slapped him hard on the butt.

"Hey!" He yelled. "Chill out with that!"

Cindy laughed and got in her Cayenne that was stuffed to the max with her things and JJ's lone suitcase, pulled away from the curb, and headed for the rally point. JJ got in his car and followed his dad out of the driveway.

Good-bye San Diego, JJ thought. *Good-bye home. Good-bye life.*

I hope this mopey attitude gets left behind too, Fire said.

"You're still an asshole."

A loveable asshole.

"But an asshole nonetheless," he sighed.

1:20 AM
Thompson Residence

A car sat running in the driveway as they approached the address he'd gotten from Google.

"Abyss," Arthur whispered, "put me down over there by her neighbor's house and be close and ready on my command."

Arthur melted through Abyss' body by the Thompson's neighbor's house and Abyss morphed into a backpack and clung tightly to his master. Arthur sensed the beast's presence but felt no physical weight from the shadow accessory.

Excellent, Arthur said in his mind, pleased with the discovery.

Someone's coming, Chaos pointed out.

It was a tall blonde woman who looked to be in the mid to late thirties. She was wearing a black leather jacket and ripped black jeans along with a pair of gothic style studded leather boots. As if her attire didn't make her look daring enough, her physique looked well enough that she could probably handle her own.

I think that's Sylvia, Arthur said to Chaos in his head.

Then go get her, Chaos aggressively suggested.

No. Look at her car.

She walked over to a silver sedan with a backseat that was packed almost to the roof with duffel bags and tote bins.

She is leaving, Chaos stated.

No, Arthur contradicted sarcastically. *I thought she was moving into her new apartment at one-something in the morning.*

Out of nowhere Arthur dropped to the ground and clawed at his head.

I will BLEED the sarcasm out of you if I have to, Chaos told him in an irritated tone.

"I'm sorry, I'm sorry, I'm sorry," Arthur apologized in a painful whisper.

Chaos stopped. Arthur raised his fingers to his ears and when he pulled them back they were wet and sticky with blood. He got up from the ground and cursed Chaos. Chaos quietly refused to acknowledge the comment.

She is driving away now, Chaos noted.
I'm on it, Arthur said and left from behind his hiding spot.

"Abyss, let's get going," Arthur ordered as he took the bag off and walked after the sedan.

He threw the bookbag on the ground between his feet and Abyss grew into his usual form with Arthur already on his back. He wasted no time following the car at a safe distance.

Get closer, Chaos advised.

"No, we're fine where we are," Arthur responded aloud.
You'll lose her.

Arthur exhaled heavily and raised his hands out in front of him. His eyes blackened as he raised his arms to the sky.

"Drop me and your existence will be extinguished," Arthur told Abyss in an unnaturally deep voice.

The sedan's shadow reached out from around the vehicle toward Arthur. He brought his hands together in the air and pretended to shoot a basketball, causing the shadow to snap quickly and quietly over the car. Arthur dropped his hands and clutched onto Abyss. His eyes returned to their natural brown color.

"Now I can sense her. Are you satisfied?" He asked Chaos.

Chaos said nothing.

"Your silence is truly a blessing."

2:15 AM
Rally Point

Anthony drove up to a cluster of cars parked as far away from the entrance as possible. He parked his escalade by the other cars and took his phone out. He called Oliver and waited until the last ring before he heard his friend's voice.

"You've only got fifteen minutes to get everything on your list," Oliver told him.

"Like speed has ever been an issue," Anthony joked.

"Just hurry up and get in here Ant," Oliver said and hung up the phone.

You have the list? Anthony asked Light.

I do, Light confirmed.

Anthony went into the Wal-Mart and grabbed a cart. He covered his eyes with his hand as they started to glow and he bent the light around himself so he'd be invisible and free to move at his own, more comfortable, speed. He zipped through the aisles and around other nearly frozen shoppers at just under light speed as Light recited the shopping list.

Shampoo, Light said.

"Got it," Anthony told him, mentally checking it off of the list.

Deodorant.

"Yep."

Soap.

"Okay, next."

Toothpaste, TP, body wash, shaving cream, razors.

"Check, check, checkity, check, check."

When they collected everything else Anthony zoomed into the bathroom, became tangible again, and casually strolled out of the bathroom with his cart of stuff. He checked his watch to see how much time was left. 2:22.

Eight minutes left.

So go pay and then mess with Ollie, Light told him.

Anthony went to one of the two open registers and paid for his $217 worth of toiletries and set off to bug his best friend. He found him in the cereal aisle throwing a bulk of Cocoa Puffs, Frosted Flakes, and Apple Jacks into his cart.

"I don't wanna eat Apple Jacks for months. Get Reese's puffs," Anthony told Oliver.

"No, I'm allergic to peanut butter, you asshat," Oliver denied and insulted.

"So just don't eat them."

"FINE!" Oliver yelled and threw several big bags of Reese's Puffs into the cart.

"Thank you," Anthony said, "let's get going. We gotta burn the midnight oil."

Oliver collected his listed items and walked to the checkout while Anthony strode beside him and talked his ear off. He paid for his own $284 worth of groceries and left the store with his best friend on his heels.

"You gonna help me put away my stuff or what?" Oliver asked when they got back to their cars.

Sylvia and Oliver's wife, Christina, were loading the remainder of Sylvia's trunk space with medical supplies, washcloths, and towels. Sylvia's car was stuffed to the top with months' worth of supplies, enough for all five families that'd be staying at CETOBA.

They had about half of Oliver's cart unloaded when they heard the furious voice of Stephanie in a screaming debate with the calm smart-assy duo that was JJ and Jericho.

"For the last freaking time, to the both of you! Oatmeal Cream Pies are *not* real food!" She shouted.

"Is *oatmeal* real food?" JJ asked in a know-it-all tone.

"Yes," she answered with her teeth noticeably clenched.

"And is *pie* real food?" Jericho asked in the same know-it-all tone.
"Yes," she answered again with her teeth still clenched.

"Sooo an Oatmeal Cream Pie is just *really* sweet, *real* food," JJ declared. "Check," he said and held up a fist to Jericho.

"Mate," Jericho said back and bumped his fist.

"ANTHONY!" Stephanie yelled.

"Yes," JJ's dad responded to her unfazed by the pair's antics, "what's the matter?"

"Your sons are insufferable," she told him.

"My son is indeed a pain in the ass but the other insufferable child, is yours."

"Don't remind me," Stephanie pleaded sarcastically.

"Steph!" Jericho yelled.

"Kidding, kidding," she defended. "Sorta," she mumbled.

JJ, Stephanie, and Jericho packed up their food into Jericho's Honda. The whole entire time doing so they pestered Stephanie until she stormed off to her car. As she slammed the door closed, Charlotte and Cindy walked over with headphones in their ears, loudly singing two different songs. They pushed their carts full of detergents, batteries, boxed electronics, fireproofing equipment, and other miscellaneous things over to the rest of the group.

"Pack up, we gotta go like now," Oliver told them.

Charlotte couldn't hear his voice over the music blaring in her ears but she read his lips and rolled her eyes.

"Sure, we'll get right on that," she said sarcastically.

"Hija!" Charlotte's mother snapped so loudly that Charlotte heard her voice through the music and snatched out her headphones. "Mind your father. Todavía no-."

"-has crecido," Charlotte finished the sentence which, of late, had become her mother's catchphrase. "I know that I'm not grown and I am not trying to be, Mama."

"Good. Now apologize to your father."

Oliver watched his wife and daughter bicker back and forth as they usually did and waited for the dust to settle.

"But mom-."

"-Pedir disculpas!"

"Sorry Papa," she apologized.

"You are forgiven bebita. Go. Pack up that stuff, we have to get a move on."

They did as they were told and packed their things into Charlotte's car before setting off.

18

THE FIGHT IN BETWEEN

◇ Wait. Do You Feel That? ◇

2:27 AM

Walmart Parking Lot

Do it now! Chaos demanded.

"Do you know how fucking stupid that would be?" Arthur asked rhetorically.

He watched Sylvia and the other woman fill the car with groceries. He sat patiently in the shadows on Abyss' back. Arthur could hear Chaos yelling demands in his mind but it was wandering elsewhere.

I haven't seen him in so long, Arthur thought to himself.

So? Chaos inquired, highly confused. ***You are here to kill him. Keep your eyes on the prize.***

"Master," Abyss said.
"What?" Arthur snapped.

"Anthony."

Arthur refocused his attention and saw him. Anthony was walking through the lot with Oliver and he appeared to be motor-mouthing the man's ear off. Arthur squinted his eyes and saw they each were carting a surplus of groceries.

"They're on the run," Arthur said aloud to Chaos.

Excellent, Chaos said, sounding pleased. ***Kill them now!***

"No. Not yet. Anthony has had his powers considerably longer than me. If I try to strike now he'd probably kill me," Arthur finished.

Chaos said nothing but Arthur sensed that It agreed with his deduction. He watched them as they heavily packed up their vehicles. He saw when JJ, Jericho, and Stephanie came out of the store arguing about snack foods. He needed the perfect moment to strike if he were to succeed. He continued watching and saw Charlotte and Cindy come out of the store singing off-key. He also saw that new kid, Zachary, and who he presumed to be his mother, walk over quietly and pack up their things. He witnessed the brief altercation between Charlotte and her mother which ended with screaming and apologies. Then, they silently finished packing up and departed.

The time is now, Chaos told Arthur.

"Indeed it is," he agreed. "Abyss."

"Master?" Abyss inquired, waiting for his commands.

"Time to kill those inconsiderate bastards."

2:45 AM
EN ROUTE TO CETOBA

Arthur followed behind them on Abyss as they quickly drove to their destination. The longer he made no move on them, the more angry and anxious Chaos became. Chaos could sense Arthur's hatred and fury and proceeded to stoke the fire.

He left you, Chaos whispered, each word scraping the inside of his skull. ***He patronized you, selfishly withheld his powers from you.***

"No that's not," he stopped and considered the possibility. "You're right."

I know, Chaos agreed. ***He refused to share his destiny with you but now, you will show him Light was destined to die!***
Arthur willed Abyss forward and Abyss erupted into a full sprint after the vehicles, throwing all stealth to the wind.

"On my signal, throw me!" Arthur commanded.

Abyss said nothing and continued on, full stride. When they were about one hundred feet away from the cars, Mr. Rodriguez got a phone call from Sylvia.

"Anthony," Sylvia called through the phone.

"What's the matter?" He asked her, noticing the concern in her voice.

"Do you feel that?"

"Yeah. It feels like thum-," he started but his phone began vibrating in his ear and he slid open a new call. "JJ?"

"Dad, do you feel that weird thumping?" JJ asked.

"Yes, get off of the phone and keep your eyes on the road," his dad told him.

He switched the call back to Sylvia and the conversation continued.

"Something's going on Anthony," Sylvia warned.

"I feel it too, just stay sharp," He instructed as he hung up, dialed Oliver and waited for him to pick up.

"Ollie, what the fuck is going on?" He asked.

"I dunno but it's getting really bumpy at the back of the bus," Oliver told him. "It's rhythmic like, like footsteps."

"What could be so damn big that its footsteps cause tremors?"

Arthur

Arthur's eyes blackened as they were a mere fifty feet away now, gaining on them fast.

"Three, two, NOW!" He signaled and was instantly launched through the air towards the cars.

This is actually kind of fun, Arthur thought as he soared.
Focus you forgetful tool, Chaos scolded.
Right. Also, shut the fuck up, he added, *because I've totally got this in the bag.*
We shall see.

Arthur was now starting to descend onto the cars, so he closed his eyes, took a deep breath, and released a deep guttural roar directly at them. A black shockwave of raw chaotic energy burst from his lips and blasted straight through two of the cars, forming a wide crater in the road. All of the cars behind them veered out of the way and off of the road to avoid the wreckage. The four cars ahead of the crater screeched to a halt as Arthur fell to the ground with Chaos in his ear.

I suggest you decide upon a course of action unless your intent was to be killed by asphalt, Chaos snidely remarked.

"Shut the fuck up," Arthur exhaled loudly. "Abyss!"

Abyss materialized out of nowhere, saddled underneath his master. A few seconds later Abyss crashed into the ground loudly and unscathed, directly in front of Anthony's car. He got off of the beast's back and stared deep into the eyes of his ex-best friend. Anthony just stared back at the man who used to be his brother, but was now nothing more than a figure of darkness shrouded in evil. Arthur gave him a short wave and then cracked open a sinister smile that his beast mimicked before he spoke.

"Hermano! What's crackin'?"

Jericho

"Dude, what the hell's happening?" Jericho asked JJ through the speakers in his car.

"I don't know," JJ's voice blared at him.

Jericho looked over into the car to his right and saw Stephanie, her face full of worry.

Air, what's going on? Jericho asked.

How the hell should I know? Air responded. *Wait. Do you feel that? That energy?*

Right after the question crossed his mind Jericho heard an insanely loud boom from overhead.

"What the fu-," was all he managed to say before something ferociously strong and deafeningly loud hit his car.

Anthony

Anthony's eyes turned yellow and his aura surrounded him as he opened his car door and got out slamming it shut behind him.

"Oh my god, JERICHO!" Someone behind him screamed at the top of their lungs.

"STEPHANIE!" Yelled somebody else.

"Arthur Arkaine," Anthony announced his opponent's presence and absentmindedly ignored the commotion behind him.

"Anthony!" Pamela shouted.

Her piercing scream diverted his attention away from the enemy and onto the wreckage. His aura immediately died away. He was absolutely mortified by the scene that lay before him. Jericho and Stephanie's cars were almost completely torn apart and disfigured, thrown about on either side of an enormous crater in the road. Car shrapnel and broken glass were scattered around them. The airbags had luckily deployed but Jericho was lying face down in his unmoving, inside what remained of his destroyed vehicle. Stephanie was out of her car, her face, neck, hands and chest terribly cut, and was limping to Jericho's part of the wreck. The others were trying to make their way over as best they could to help.

"Cindy! JJ! Charlotte!" Anthony yelled. "On me!"

They're not ready yet Anthony!" Charlotte's mom protested.

Anthony didn't respond. He turned back to Arkaine who was just staring at him, patiently waiting.

"They have no choice but to be," he said so loudly and sternly that he didn't receive any more protests from anybody. "The rest of you tend to Jericho and Stephanie."

After a moment of nobody moving and unwavering silence, Oliver spoke up.

"You heard what he said. Move!" He yelled and they scurried to help the wounded while the others joined Anthony.

"Arthur, think about this," Anthony pleaded, although his tone and the ignition of his aura indicated that it was less of a request than a warning.

"Okay, gimme a sec," Arkaine requested in a playful manner.

'What's cracking' is neither evil nor sinister, Chaos informed him, sounding slightly more irritated than usual.
Good, Arkaine said blandly.
Good?!
I'm not evil or sinister.
Then please enlighten me as to what you are.
I am the Keeper of Chaos!

Chaos said nothing but Arkaine felt his aura strengthen. His shadowy aura thrashed around him erratically.

"Your request has been submitted," Arkaine chimed. "DENIED!"

Anthony took a step forward and his eyes normalized and his aura melted away.

"*Tu eres mi familia,*" Anthony said, trying to convince the part of Arthur that used to be his brother, but no longer existed within Arkaine.

"Don't patronize me!" Arkaine screamed.

"I have no family!" Chaos and Arkaine shouted together through Arkaine's mouth in a disturbingly twisted amalgamation of voices. "But at least today's the last day I ever have to put up with your intolerable existence."

Anthony's eyes immediately lit back up and his aura jumped to life around him. He understood that no matter what he said or did, this altercation was far beyond heartfelt sentiments.

"False," Fire said through JJ's mouth. "Today's the day you die, Chaos."

"We shall see," Chaos shot back unflinchingly.

He clapped his hands together in JJ's direction and a dark energy pulse shot from his hands into JJ's chest. He was thrown straight backwards into the air and less than a second later, into a car. Fortunately, only his legs connected with the car. Unfortunately, that caused him to somersault through the air until he inevitably smacked into the asphalt below. Mr. Rodriguez looked horrified at Charlotte through his glowing yellow eyes.

"Go check on him please," he begged.

"On it," she told him and rushed off with intense urgency.

"Cindy," Anthony said, his gaze never leaving Arkaine's.

"Yes?" She asked with the slightest reservation in her voice.

"You're probably gonna need a weapon for this next part."

She smiled to herself and quickly concentrated on making a weapon for herself. Her aura moved around her hands wickedly and she knew exactly what she was going to make.

Be careful my Elementalist, Earth warned.

When am I not? Cindy asked sarcastically.

The aura solidified around her hands and she stared at Mr. Rodriguez beaming.

"How's this?" She asked, clearly proud of her work.

Anthony looked over at her and saw her hands wrapped up in two bulging bouldery gauntlets surrounded by a radical swarm of elemental energy. He smiled at her.

"That'll do just fine," he told her as blistering white halos of light the size of dinner plates formed in his clenched hands, his own elemental energy audibly crackling around them.

Those always were your favorite for close-quarter combat, Light reminisced.

They're efficient, he told Light.

Adrenaline started pumping through Cindy's veins and that warm fuzzy feeling filled up her insides. This was finally her chance to show up to the showdown and show out. The fact that the person she was being given permission to pummel was the teacher she just happened to absolutely abhor at the moment well, to her, that was nothing but icing on the cake.

"Oh fuck yeah! Let's do this!" She shouted and slammed her gauntlets together, her eagerness refusing to be contained.

"Cindy!" Anthony yelled to get her attention and try to center her on the gravity of the situation.

"Yeah?"

"Let's fuck him up," he ordered through a dangerously wicked smile.

Jericho

Jericho could barely open his eyes. His body stung all over. He couldn't really hear anything but, he was sure that the taste in his mouth was blood. More blood than a person ever really wants to taste.

Air? Jericho managed to call weakly into his mind.

Jericho! Air called back immediately, the concern practically palpable. *I'm here.*

Help me.

I will try.

Jericho's eyes lit up and all of his senses snapped back on in full effect, like someone reset his internal breaker. Now that he had a full grasp on his senses, he realized that he was definitely tasting blood. *Bad sign.* He swallowed hard and the coppery taste slid down his throat but stuck to his taste buds. He took a brief second to look around and only then did he realize why he was in so much pain.

"We crashed?" Jericho voiced the question aloud.

"Unlikely," Air responded through his mouth. "The road was open and we don't remember seeing any animals."

"So, what? We were-."

"-hit, more than likely."

Jericho looked around again as best he could and saw he was wedged into the seat by the car's crushed metal.

"We've gotta get outta here," Jericho said to Air.

"Sounds like you've got a plan."

"You know I do, we share the same mental space."

Conversation ceased and Jericho closed his eyes and listened intently. Around him he heard a bit of commotion, metal scraping and voices, but in the distance he heard another loud boom, similar to the original one, followed by something hitting metal. Hard.

"Hello?" Jericho yelled as loud as he could.

"Jericho!" Stephanie yelled back. "He's over there!" She yelled to someone near her. "I'm coming baby!"

"No!" Jericho shouted. "Back up from the car and get in a safe place to avoid any flying shrapnel!"

"But-" Stephanie protested.
"-Trust me! Please, just trust me!"

There was a brief moment of quiet from outside of the car.

"We're safe! Do it now!" She yelled.

Jericho exhaled heavily and took in an unnaturally long deep breath. Air counted off the seconds in his head.

Twelve. Thirteen. Fourteen. Fifteen. Sixteen. Seventeen. Eighteen. Nineteen, Air counted.

When Air reached the count of twenty, Jericho opened his hands and all of the air he'd been storing and pressurizing in his lungs exploded from his palms. The compression burst blasted the car apart, causing glass and metal to scatter every which way. Jericho opened his eyes and saw the destruction he'd caused. He managed to free himself although he did shatter Mr. Santiago's back windshield and impaled Mrs. Thompson's car with a jagged piece of car door.

"Necessary," Jericho reassured himself.

Stephanie peeked out from behind the wreckage that was her car and tears cascaded down her face. Jericho sprinted over to her and hugged her tight. He looked her in her foggy gray-green eyes and his eyes stopped glowing and his aura dissipated.

"I love you Steph," Jericho said with tears in his eyes.

"I love you too, ya big softy," she replied as she wiped his tears away. "Now light those eyes back up, you've got work to do," she told him and pointed to the ongoing fight between JJ's dad, Cindy, Arkaine and his beasts.

"What the hell is that?" Jericho asked her, referring to the eight-foot tall black monster standing in the background.

"A shadow beast. No more questions. GO!"

Jericho's eyes ignited back up and his aura flared around him as he lifted up off of the ground and glided towards battle.

Let's go kick some ass, Air told him.

Jericho silently agreed. Right before he reached the fight he saw Charlotte off to the side nursing JJ back to health. He landed by them and startled Charlotte.

"Boy!" She shrieked. "Don't sneak up on people like that!" She warned him with glowing blue eyes.

"Sorry," he apologized, extinguishing his aura. "What's wrong with JJ," he paused, "you know, besides the arm."

JJ had a cut on the middle of the back of his right forearm that ran just short of the elbow. His blood was all over the road.

"I closed the cut so that's dealt with but Arkaine blasted him over Cindy's dad's car," she told him as her eyes normalized.

"Damn, is he good?"

"I mean he flipped and shit but I don't think anything's broken or fractured. He's definitely bruised but he'll live."

"Right here guys," JJ spoke up, "right here."

"Char, go help Pops and Cindy," Jericho instructed.

She got up, her eyes turning blue and her aura swooshing around her as she did so, then took off to help with the fight. Jericho reached down and helped JJ to his feet.

"You good?" Jericho asked him.

"Me? Yeah. Dude your car got fucked up, are *you* good?" He asked back, noticing the many cuts and bloodstains displayed all across his friend's attire.

"Not really, but I will be. Let's go kick some ass," Jericho told him as his eyes lit up again.

He held his fist out to JJ.

"That sounds like a plan," Fire said as JJ's eyes burned red and his aura thrashed all around him.
JJ met his fist bump and they gave each other a quick hug. They fully understood the situation they were in. They were Elementalists. Their least favorite teacher was now a supervillain that they had no choice but to deal with, whatever that may entail. And no matter how they tried to swing it, left or right, this was their life now. Jericho rose into the air and took off towards the battle with JJ running behind him.

Charlotte

Charlotte rushed off to help defend her family by defeating Arkaine and Chaos. Cindy was on a rock hoverboard with rocky gauntlets punching down anything that got too close to her. Mr. Rodriguez was powering through wave after wave of beasts while also fending off the giant beast that Arkaine rode in on. Arkaine was busy using all of his energy conjuring enough beasts to swarm them both.

Damn, this looks bad, Charlotte confessed to Water.

True, She agreed. *Although, your presence combined with those boys' should make a tangible difference in this battle and could very well be the turning tide,* Water told Charlotte.

Knowing Water had so much faith in her and her friends gave Charlotte some much needed hope, so she steeled herself and focused.

Water, I need your help, she pleaded.

Always, Water told her.

Charlotte raised her hands into the air and concentrated on an image of throwing knives in her head. Slowly the aura around her hands began to swirl, stretch out in front of her, and take shape. When the knives formed the water wasn't clear like it'd been when she'd first used her powers at CETOBA, it was whitewater, like the rapids she constantly visited as a child. Six knives hovered in front of her and each looked plenty sharp for the task at hand.

"This'll do," she said to herself and thrust her hands forward as hard as she could, shooting them at Arkaine like homing missiles.

Not even a second before they were going to stab him to death, he looked up. Quicker than the blink of an eye, he summoned a beast directly in front of himself and it was instantly impaled by the six elemental blades. It erupted into thick shadowy smoke and the knives clattered to the ground before splashing into nothingness. Arkaine screamed and a dense chaotic shockwave spread across the battlefield, causing all of his beasts to be destroyed and knocking all of his opponents to the ground. Cindy crashed into the ground and her hoverboard smashed into pieces.

"Char-lotte," Arkaine and Chaos called out to her in an eerie sing-song voice. "Didn't your parents ever teach you not to play with knives?"

As his voice crept toward her a pure black knife formed in his hand, identical to the ones she'd just tried to assassinate him with. He took slow steps toward her but a plume of fire burst against the ground in front of him. He snapped his head in the direction of the warning shot and saw JJ standing a few yards away dead-eyeing him through glowing red eyes. He had a snarl on his face and his fists were on fire, ready and waiting for Arkaine to challenge him.

"Justin," they addressed him and smiled like they were old friends. "I always said you were a hothead."

Arkaine's knife elongated into a sword and he ran at JJ.

"Abyss! Handle the rest!" Arkaine howled.

Abyss sprang into action, splitting into four copies of itself and trying to kill the others, as commanded. Anthony pulled Cindy to her feet and she saw what challenge lay ahead. She looked down at her gauntlets, they'd become cracked and chipped. A few of the fingers on her left hand had become exposed and were coated in her own blood. She closed her eyes for a quick second and her aura wrapped around her old gauntlets, solidifying a whole new layer of thicker denser rock atop the first.

"Okay second layer. Let's do this," she said as she cocked her arm back and slammed a rocky fist into the charging Abyss' face.

JJ

"Always hated you as a teacher," JJ taunted as he threw multiple balls of fire at Arkaine.

Arkaine dodged and sliced through them with his sword and purged on. JJ was playing the most intense game of Chess he'd ever played in his life, his moves and countermoves were literally the determining factors of whether he lived or died. Arkaine swung the sword across at his head and he dropped to the ground like a corpse, sending a torrent of fire at his stomach in return. Arkaine sidestepped the flames and stabbed at JJ. He rolled back and forth to avoid being stabbed, and jumped back up to his feet. For a brief moment JJ was one step ahead of Arkaine and managed to catch him off guard. He swung his fist as hard as he could into Arkaine's jaw and cracked him hard, making him stumble backwards a few steps. He spit a glob of blood onto the ground and stared at JJ with his deep black eyes.

"That is the only one you'll get, Keeper of Fire," Chaos declared with so much hate and anger that JJ took a couple of steps back himself, as if the words themselves could harm him.

Anthony finally killed the largest of the Abysses with his light discs and teleported to his son's side. JJ jumped out of his skin at the unexpected appearance of his father.

"Holy shit! You scared me," JJ told his dad. "I think I peed a little."

"First, gross. Second, after all of this is said and done, we're gonna discuss your language," his dad said back.

"Cool," JJ agreed nonchalantly.

Arkaine was upon them incredibly fast and he wasted no time.

Kill them, Chaos demanded as Arkaine swung the sword.

Anthony deflected the sword with a disc of light and the sword impaled the ground. Arkaine stared at the sword, then the disc, then at Anthony. He smiled as he looked Anthony in his bright yellow eyes.

"Shit happens," he joked before Anthony slashed his face with a disc.

"Indeed it does," Anthony remarked as Arkaine pulled his sword free.

Arkaine and Anthony swung intense blows at each other with their elemental weapons, each of them knowing that a single miscalculation in strength and accuracy could be the death of them. With his father having the fight well in hand, JJ rushed off to help Jericho defeat his Abyss. Jericho was throwing air kunai at the monster and flying up and away from the beast's reach. JJ's aura flared wildly around him as he threw torrents of flames at the beast while Jericho continued throwing his razor sharp kunai. Seemingly out of nowhere, Zach was beside them with glowing orange eyes and an orange aura flaring around him. He cracked the earth around him and summoned liquid magma from somewhere beneath. He stepped into the lava and it climbed up his legs, over his back, and across his arms impossibly quick. He opened his palms and blasted rapid bursts of magma at the Abyss like a gatling gun.

Charlotte was to the left of them battling the smallest of the Abysses, but also the quickest. She was forming javelin poles, stabbing and throwing them at the beast. The Abyss already had three poles sticking out of its body, one in the bottom of its neck, one in the side of its back, and one in its hind leg. It simply ignored all of its injuries and continued its pursuit of death. Behind her, Cindy was sailing through the air on a giant flat boulder pecking punches at the Abyss she was fighting. Whenever her gauntlets cracked or chipped she just replaced it with a new layer and kept fighting.

Forget the monster, Fire told JJ. *Kill Arkaine while he's distracted.*

JJ looked over at his dad who was exchanging blows with Arkaine. His dad had a cut on the side of his stomach, yet he still persevered. He looked tired but showed no sign of stopping, nor did Arkaine. This was a bout to the death.

But what if I hit dad? JJ considered.
Fifty, fifty. Risk it!
You're right. You're right. Besides, dad can teleport.

Exactly. Do it now!

JJ's aura crackled in his hands and formed a fiery dory, a spartan era spear. Arkaine caught him in his peripheral and whistled unnaturally loud, never breaking concentration from the altercation at hand. JJ cocked his arms back to launch the fatal blow but a jagged, misshapen shadow copy of himself lurched up from beneath his feet and pinned him to the ground.

"Get off of me you evil puppet," Fire growled.

"Kill him!" Arkaine ordered while sidestepping a swing from a light disc that would've spilled his guts on the ground.

Anthony knew this battle could rage on forever if he didn't end it and his team, as valiant as they were, simply couldn't continue fighting forever. He needed to end the fight and get them to safety. He needed an opening to end it all. Arkaine swung a hefty blow at Anthony's legs and created exactly the opening he was looking for.

Anthony. Are you sure you can do this? Light asked, more cautious than concerned.

There's no time for second guessing or weighing my options, he said back. *It's now or never.*

Anthony knew the maneuver he was going to attempt was risky but it had to be done. He backflipped into the air and the next few moments passed by in slow motion. As his left hand hit the ground, he felt the tip of the shadowy blade swooshing by his head.

That was close, he thought.

Focus, Light chastised.

He redirected his attention onto his son who was being mauled by a shadow clone. He opened his palm toward the doppelganger and a searing beam of light exploded from it, forming a frisbee sized hole in the imposter. Anthony pushed himself to his feet and turned to see his son's crude double evaporate into nothingness. A smile beamed across his face until his eyes landed on his son, who was writhing on the ground in agony. His face had been clawed to hell and a fire raged inside of Anthony.

"Aaaaugh!" Arkaine screamed as he swung the sword down onto Anthony's head.

Just before the weapon made contact Anthony's aura wrapped around him and overloaded, blasting into Arkaine and sending him flying head over heels into the distance. He teleported to his son's side but Charlotte's voice diverted his attention.

"We could use a little help," she shrieked.

Mr. Rodriguez looked up and saw the others battling for their lives against the shadow beasts. He took a deep breath and concentrated his energy. He shot intense beams of light at the beasts evaporating them, two at a time. For moments everyone was at rest except for JJ, who was crying out in agony and his father, who was worrying about his condition.

"Everyone! Come here!" Anthony shouted, including his friends and their respective partners.

They all crowded him as Arkaine got up in the distance.

"Join hands and take a deep breath," Anthony instructed them.

We've never transferred this many people at once before, Light warned.

WHAT CHOICE DO WE HAVE? Anthony screamed into his mind.

Arkaine landed hard on his stomach but refused to be stopped. He raised a hand quickly into the air and the shadows of nearby trees conjoined into a thick disfigured horse. He climbed on its back as he caught his breath and began charging back to the fight at full speed. He was about fifty feet away when his eyes met Anthony's as he reached down to touch his son's stomach.

"This is only the beginning," Light yelled at Arkaine.

"How right you are," Chaos yelled back as the whole group disappeared in a flash of light.

Arkaine's aura strengthened and he shouted as loud as inhumanly possible.

"FIND THEM!" He yelled so loudly it seemed to echo through the cosmos.

19

THIS IS THE SAFEST THING

◇ Prepare For The War Ahead ◇

4:17 AM

Outside CETOBA

Anthony, JJ, Charlotte, Oliver, Christina, Jericho, Stephanie, Cindy, Sylvia, Hector, Zach, and Pamela

They tumbled onto the scorching sand of the freezing nighttime desert gasping for air. Anthony wasn't one hundred percent sure he'd gotten everyone to safety, but he knew he'd tried to.

"Light do a headcount," Anthony wheezed.

Twelve, Light told him.

Anthony exhaled a sigh of relief.

"Everyone! Quickly follow me, we have to get inside," Anthony insisted.

He scooped his son into his arms and rushed up to the secret base as quickly as he could.

"CETOBA!" Anthony yelled. "SUBITIS!

"Voice pattern recognized," AVA announced. "Emergency entry code activated. How many entries?" AVA asked.

"Twelve. Once we're inside, initiate extreme lockdown protocol," he told her.

"Understood."

The twelve of them rushed into CETOBA and the doors slammed shut.

"Initiating extreme lockdown protocol in three, two, one," AVA announced and the building started to shake vigorously.

"What's going on?" Jericho yelled.

"The protocol dumbass. Pay attention," Charlotte told him.

They endured two long minutes of quaking before the building settled.

"What just happened?" Stephanie asked Anthony.

"All seven stories of the building are now underground," he explained to everyone. "For now, this is the safest thing."

JJ lay in his father's arms unmoving, except for his chest that was barely showing he was still breathing.

"He needs medical attention," Pamela said frantically.

"I know," Anthony told her. "I'm on it."

He teleported himself and JJ to the med bay and sat JJ down on the sick bed. At this point the pain had forced him into unconsciousness. He put an IV into his son's arm and a heart monitor on his finger. Anthony leaned in close to his son and lightly kissed him on the forehead.

"You're gonna be okay," he whispered to his son as the monitor beeped. "I love you Justin."

He reached into a drawer on the stand beside the bed and grabbed out a large roll of gauze. As gently as possible, Anthony began wrapping his son's bloodied almost unrecognizable face in gauze, uncontrollable tears streaming down his face as he completed the task. He put an oxygen tube in his son's nose, knelt down beside the bed and continued crying. The others eventually found their way and trickled quietly into the room. Charlotte stared down at JJ's face all wrapped up and tears welled up in her eyes.

"Is he gonna be okay?" Charlotte whispered.

"I don't know," Mr. Rodriguez confessed quietly. "I don't know."

She sniffled and turned away from her friend.

"Okay," she said so quietly it was barely audible.

Her mother hugged her tightly. Charlotte just cried quietly into her mom's shirt. Cindy and Jericho both went to get a closer look at JJ and couldn't help but be overcome with sadness for their friend and brother.

"Let's get you all fixed up," Sylvia said to them with false bravado. "We might've survived that battle and as intense as it was, it was nowhere near the war."

The three of them got patched up by their parents as Anthony knelt beside his son crying. They got taken care of and headed towards their rooms to rest after a long day of fighting and stressing.

"What the fuck are we gonna do?" Anthony asked Light as he wiped his tears away, finally alone.

Prepare for the war ahead, Light suggested hesitantly.

Anthony's visage hardened. In this moment, he knew he didn't have the luxury of mourning because he had to lead his family to victory. They were continuing the cycle of Light versus Chaos and Light had to prevail, no matter the stakes. But even more importantly, he had to train these new Elementalists to be even better than their predecessors because as he stood there over his son, he knew he could never allow this to happen again.

"Prepare for the war ahead," Anthony repeated.

TRANSLATIONS

Chapter 4:
Lo mío es tuyo, lo tuyo es mío - What's mine is yours, what's yours is mine

Chapter 5:
Señor - Mister

Chapter 10:
C'est la vie - Such is life
Excelente - Excellent

Chapter 14:
A veces los inocentes deben morir - Sometimes the innocent must die

Chapter 17:
Hija – Daughter
Todavía no has crecido –

You have not yet grown
Pedir disculpas - Apologize
Bebita - Baby girl

18:

Tu eres mi familia - You are my family

Keep Reading To Find Out What Happens Next
In The Legend of the Core - The Core
Elementalists Book 2: The Trials of Fire

20

EIGHTY-FOUR DAYS
◇ Let Me Think, Uh, Duh! ◇

9:30 AM
CETOBA's Med Bay

Today was the day that JJ had been waiting for, for the last eighty-four days. He was more excited than he ever thought possible and with the Fire elemental screaming in his mind, he knew that he wasn't the only one.

Eighty-four! Fire shouted inside of JJ's head. *We finally get to take these stupid stinking bandages off of our face after eighty-four never-ending days!*

They're on my face dude, JJ kindly informed his Elemental counterpart.

Your face, my face, our face, thee face! The bandages are coming off somebody's stinking face! I swear to the Core Being I'm excited!

Oh you're excited? JJ asked sarcastically. *I couldn't tell.*

Wouldn't think you'd have such an attitude since not too long ago Arkaine turned your face into mincemeat, Fire remarked but instantly regretted it. *I'm so sorry, my Elementalist,* Fire apologized. *There's a line and I crossed it. Please forgive me.*

It's fine, JJ said calmly. *For almost three months we've been cooped up inside of my head and I know we're both a little cramped.*

"Let's get these bandages off already dad," JJ said aloud to his father who was going to finally remove the bandages from his face permanently.

JJ, Charlotte, Jericho, and Zach laughed. His best friends had come to visit JJ every opportunity they had gotten in between training and missions. They ate in the room with him and on most occasions slept in there too. Now today was the day that JJ would be liberated from his bandages, and they wouldn't miss it for the world.

"Justin, mind your manners," his dad told him, clearly exhausted from having to constantly repeat this phrase over and over. "And you four," he paused and waved a finger at the group of gigglers, "stop hyping him up."

Zach's face scrunched up as if he'd bit into a lemon as he heard the words 'hyping him up' leave the grown man's lips.

"Hyping him up?" Zach asked, a little bit of disgust biting the edge of the question. "Really?"

"My slang's getting better right?" Mr. Rodriguez asked with a huge grin on his face.

Zach started to respond negatively but caught Charlotte staring daggers into him and reluctantly changed his answer.

"Sure man, whatever you say."

"Excellent! Now, are you ready?" JJ's dad asked him.

"Let me think, uh, duh!" JJ responded.

"Again, manners."

JJ and Fire were becoming more impatient by the second.

"Just take the damn bandages off Anthony!" Fire demanded, speaking through JJ's mouth.

"Please," JJ added.

> ***He did ask politely***, Light said to Anthony in his mind.
> ***Fire didn't***, Anthony said back.
> ***Well, he's a little hot tempered.***
> ***That'll never be funny, I swear.***
> ***One of these days you'll laugh at it.***

Mr. Rodriguez gently lifted his son's head and found the spot where the bandages ended. Slowly he began unwrapping his son's head, as if he were trying to carefully unmask a mummy. JJ sat there buzzing in his skin, anxious to be freed from his head swaddled prison.

"Ahh!" JJ shouted as the light hit his eyes for the first time in months.

"You're dramatic," Charlotte told him. "It's super freaking dark in here."

"To you, maybe," JJ said feeling insulted, "but to someone who's seen nothing but darkness for the past couple of months it's kind of bright."

JJ looked at his friends and smiled. It'd been so long since he'd seen their faces and he just couldn't help himself. Even seeing Zach, who he'd barely known before moving to the secret base, made him smile harder than he'd ever naturally smiled before.

"You okay?" Cindy asked JJ. "You kind of look like the Grinch when he decided he was gonna steal the Who's Christmas."

"I'm happy," JJ told her. "I get to see again."

His dad picked up a small flashlight and began to check JJ's eyes. After he cleared the test, Mr. Rodriguez picked up a mirror from off of the side table and sat on the bed beside his son. He looked directly into his eyes and spoke.

"Justin. You're about to see yourself for the first time in a long time and, as your father, I'm going to tell you that it may take some getting used to, seeing yourself like this," his dad explained. "As a person, I'm going to tell you that you don't look exactly like you used to. There's some scarring all over your face so I'm going to hand you this," he paused and handed JJ the mirror face down, "and you take your time and look when you're ready."

JJ stared over at the others and for a second he felt as if they'd see him as a disfigured monster and avoid his gaze like the plague. To his surprise, none of their gazes swayed and they all looked right back at him in a cautious but tender way. They all understood the severity of the moment. During an egregious assault by Arkaine, the bearer of the Chaos Elemental, and his hell-raising shadow beasts, Arkaine had conjured a shadow clone that had clawed up JJ's face and put him into a two and a half week coma. Since he'd woken up sixty-seven days ago his face had been wrapped in bandages and he'd only seen darkness. Looking into the mirror he held in his hand was a monumental milestone in his journey as an Elementalist. JJ knew that this moment would also test his internal strength.

Can I live with the person I see in my reflection? He asked himself.

You're stuck with the man in the mirror, Fire chipped in.

JJ chuckled to himself and, as quietly as he could think it, whined, *hee-hee*, at Fire's Michael Jackson reference.

He took a deep breath and Fire counted down in his mind.

Three, Fire whispered. *Two. One.*

JJ flipped the mirror in his hands and stared into the eyes of his reflection. The damage hit him all at once. From his forehead all the way down to his chin, thick reddish-tan scars laced their way up and down and left and right, all over his face. He raised his hand to his face and gently touched the longest scar on his face. It started on his forehead, above and to the right of his left eyebrow, almost directly in the middle. He traced it a little ways down the protrusion of his nose, underneath his eye, and onto his cheek. Another scar intersected and kept it running down his cheek towards his mouth where it trailed off on his chin, just underneath his lips. He continued touching all of the scars, making a mental map of their location on his face. It was literally the worst network of lines he'd ever had the displeasure of tracing.

The room stayed quiet and patient as JJ carefully and meticulously examined his face. He traced the scars with such intent and precision that he seemed to lose himself in the process. Countless minutes passed before JJ finally finished and put the mirror face down onto the bed. He closed his eyes and took a few deep breaths before looking up at everyone. He watched them watch him, waiting to hear whatever he had to say so they could act accordingly. He wanted to tell them he was fine and everything was okay, yet, he found that he could only be silent. He got up from the bed and hugged his father. The room seemed to ease a little until JJ's eyes lit up and his aura raged around him.

"JJ?" His dad said his name, questioning who he needed to address.

"No," Fire said uncharacteristically quiet through JJ's mouth.

"Where's JJ?" Charlotte said concerned as she stood up and walked toward him.

"He's, wait," Fire paused, "spending some time, in, the background."

"What does that mean?"

"I'm only telling you, what he's telling me," Fire explained. "He says for now he doesn't want to talk to anybody, he just wants time to readjust."

Jericho exhaled heavily and hadn't even realized he'd been holding his breath.

"He's fine. He did this all the time before he was bonded with Fire, just give him some time and he'll be back to norm-," Jericho was cut off by his own Elemental.

"-himself," Air clarified.

"Yeah," Jericho jumped back in, "himself."

"He's in control of his body so any physical interactions are still his doing, I'm just the voice he's projecting with," Fire explained.

Mr. Rodriguez walked to the med bay doors and cleared his throat.

"How about some breakfast then some training?" He suggested.

"Sounds good."

10:30 AM
Elemental Training Arena

After they'd eaten and had time to digest an incredibly filling meal of Wheaties and orange juice, they headed to the Elemental Training Arena, formerly known as the Elemental Training Area. The name was changed after the battle with Arkaine. Coincidentally that's also when the one day of somewhat lackadaisical training turned into an everyday routine of intense physical, mental, and spiritual regiments. His friends would come in after practices and explain the intensity of the workout. In some cases when they were too tired, their Elementals would explain it to him so they could rest. Needless to say, JJ wasn't entirely pumped for the workout.

JJ's father led them into the Arena and without hesitation Jericho, Zach, Charlotte, and Cindy began stretching. JJ followed their lead and began copying their stretches. After twenty minutes of limbering up, Mr. Rodriguez gave them instructions.

"Phase through and assume formation Delta Seven," he told them. "No Elements for now, just combat."

Everyone who knew what the instructions meant did as they were told. Their eyes lit up and their auras calmly swayed around them. They took their stances and began practicing, throwing punches and kicks at one another free-for-all style. JJ's father turned to him and stared right into his son's glowing eyes. He took a deep breath.

"Justin," he said, still trying to hear from his son.

"No. Still Fire," Fire told him.

"I want to talk to my son!" Mr. Rodriguez demanded a little too loudly.

Practice halted for a split second before immediately picking back up. They'd all witnessed firsthand how powerful JJ's dad was and how unstable he could become when upset. Right after JJ's accident Mr. Rodriguez went into a deep state of sadness. He wouldn't eat anything and he would only sleep when his body forced him to. He stopped socializing with everyone including Charlotte's dad Oliver, his best friend. The only time he talked was when he went to the Elemental Training Arena, set up dummies, and yelled at them as he obliterated them all with incredible displays of power. He seemed to get out his anger and frustration that way but soon after he'd finished, he'd always go back to the same sad reflection of himself. It got better when JJ got out of his coma because he was talkative and seemingly himself. That morning, when JJ vowed his silence and Fire took over the speaking role, Anthony seemed to slip back into his dark place. At breakfast nobody wanted to test him to see where he was at. The same unspoken caution was to continue during practice.

"JJ says he doesn't want to talk now but he will follow whatever directions you have for him," Fire explained as JJ's body stood motionless.

"Alright," Anthony said discontentedly to Fire.

His eyes lit up and his aura buzzed all around him. He cupped his hands and his aura began spinning above his hands until it turned into a white sphere of rotating light the size of a billiards ball.

"Plea-please," he stopped and cleared his throat. "Please do the same."

JJ cupped his hands just like his father's and concentrated on making a ball of fire. Even though he was riding in the backseat of his mind, he could still control his powers just the same. His aura spiraled around his arms and pooled in his hands. Less than a second later a fiery white hot ball was hovering above JJ's hands and he just looked back up at his father awaiting the next direction.

"Impressive considering the amount of time you haven't used your powers," his dad praised him. "Now throw it at me."

Without hesitation JJ threw the fire at his father. Mr. Rodriguez' sphere of light expanded and inhaled JJ's ball of fire.

"Elemental absorption is a critical skill when fighting Chaos because there will surely be attacks more powerful than you can deflect or avoid," he explained to his son. "He will only get more powerful and we don't want any mishaps the next time around. Now make another fireball and get ready to do the same."

JJ followed the instructions and continued going back and forth throwing and absorbing attacks for the next thirty-minutes.

This is getting tedious, JJ told Fire, who relayed the message.

"Is he tired yet?" Mr. Rodriguez asked.

"Yes, he thought that was implied in the tedious complaint," Fire answered.

"Alright," he yelled to everyone, "regroup so we can practice conjuring.

They dropped everything and did as they were told. They formed a circle and, all at once, their auras frantically thrashed around them. Mr. Rodriguez made them go through the motions of conjuring their elements in their hands over and over. It only took about ten minutes for Cindy to get bored and protest.
"Ugh," she grumbled.

"Something on your mind?" Mr. Rodriguez asked with a touch of annoyance behind the inquiry.

"This is boring," she moaned.

"Pray tell, what would you like to do instead?"

"I would like to practice, um, advanced travel," she said, enunciating as much of the last two words as possible.

Everyone except Fire laughed at her request. She only asked about it a hundred times every practice and expressly told all of them that it was her favorite thing to do.

"Who could've guessed?" Mr. Rodriguez asked sarcastically. "Let's get through conjuring drills and then we can have a race or something," he told her.

"Awesome possum," she responded.

"Ugh, you're killing me Cee," Zach said jokingly. "You're killing me."

For the next thirty minutes they performed drill after conjuring drill and JJ noticed something different about Zach's powers. He bonded with the Magma Core so JJ had assumed that his friend would wield lava as his weapon. He did, but in addition to lava, he could also create molten rocks and he made it a mission to copy Cindy, because it seemed to get under her skin that he could perfectly replicate her moves. JJ wanted to talk to Zach and his friends and his father but, at the same time, he didn't really want to talk to anybody. He felt so conflicted. His feelings were two sides of a coin, so close, yet they were so impossibly far away. So he said nothing and continued on with the drills.

"Alright that's enough practice for now," Mr. Rodriguez declared. "Who wants to race?"

"Oooh that sounds like music to my ears," Cindy mused.

Wasting no time at all, she concentrated her tan aura around her feet and it circled around her in a wild display of excitement. She looked down at the solid gray clay boots she'd created around her feet. Cindy stretched her hands out in front of her and her aura condensed in front of her. It widened and flattened out before solidifying with a loud CRUNCH! She slowly lowered the five foot slab of granite before gently placing it on the ground. She stepped on to it and began fusing the boots and the board together. As she was doing that, Charlotte was talking with Mr. Rodriguez about the race.

"I think I'm gonna sit this one out," Charlotte told him.

"That's fine," he responded. "Is everything okay?"

"Yes, with me, but not with JJ. I want to see if I can reach him."

"Do what you have to," he said softly and touched her arm tenderly.

Charlotte invited JJ and Fire over to the chairs in the back of the room and they took a seat as the race began. Cindy, Zach, Jericho, and Mr. Rodriguez were all lined up in the corner of the room. Zach continued the mimicry and made his own molten rock hoverboard, it's glowing orange veins continually moving around beneath him. Jericho's aura twirled around him in an intense funnel, making him look as if he were riding a tornado. Mr. Rodriguez's aura just swayed calmly, as if he weren't even concerned with his competitors.

"Ready!" Charlotte began the countdown. "Set!"

A split second before the next word left her lips, she made her hand into a finger gun and her aura wrapped it, forming a watery starter pistol.

"Go!" She yelled and the pistol fired off loudly, spraying her with a light mist.

They all sped off impossibly fast and began lapping the whole arena. Charlotte looked over at JJ and began talking to Fire.

"Hey hot head," she joked.

A few seconds passed and Fire didn't say anything, it just stared at Charlotte blankly. It took what Charlotte thought was too many moments to pass before Fire said anything.

"He didn't respond," Fire told her.

"Juss? You in there?" She asked, desperately trying to reach JJ.

"He says he can hear you."

"I don't want to hear it from you, no offense. I wanna hear from my friend."

"Damn, I thought we were friends," Fire said, outright offended.

"I didn't mean it like," she just trailed off. "My bad Fire," she apologized, "I just miss JJ is all."

"I figured."

The racers whooshed to an abrupt stop in the corner of the room where the race began. Charlotte was incredibly grateful for the escape from awkward conversation. Mr. Rodriguez was first, then Cindy, followed by Zach and Jericho coming in last but tying for third.

To no one's surprise Cindy was pissed that she hadn't come in first and made a big spectacle about losing. Zach laughed and poked fun at her rage which triggered one of he and Cindy's daily brawls that broke out periodically during the day. He was, as Cindy so elegantly put it, the wasp that continued to repeatedly sting you over and over. While they fought with each other Mr. Rodriguez came over to check on Charlotte's progress.

"Don't kill each other!" Jericho yelled at the competitors as JJ's dad walked away from the commotion.

"Charlotte," he beckoned her over, just a couple feet away from where JJ was sitting. "Any luck at all?" he asked quietly.

"I'm sorry. He's just locked himself away and I don't think he's gonna come out until he wants to," she tried to explain.

She looked up into his eyes and they were drenched in an overwhelming sadness. She felt so clueless. How was she supposed to comfort this man who was like a second father to her, when she herself was experiencing the same thing? The same pain. The same exact helplessness. After what felt like an eternity of silence had passed between them, Mr. Rodriguez finally spoke.

"What are we supposed to do?" He asked, directing the question to no one in particular. It was simply just a cry for help.

Charlotte reached up and wiped the tears from her uncle's cheeks and smiled at him.
"We wait."

This is a work of fiction. The characters, incidents, and most locations portrayed and the names herein are fictitious, and any similarity to or identification with the location, name, character or history of any person, product, or entity is entirely coincidental and unintentional.